Borderline Freaks MC #2

MariaLisa deMora

Edited by Hot Tree Editing

Proofreading by Whiskey Jack Editing

First Published 2019

ISBN 13: 978-1-946738-47-9

DEDICATION

Valor is stability, not of legs and arms, but of courage and the soul. ~ Michel de Montaigne

To those who feel bent and broken,
there is hope for us all.

Contents

ACKNOWLEDGMENTS

In this book, I loved exploring how Blade personifies so many pieces of what are innate human characteristics. Few of us believe we're worthy, no matter the challenges faced. Most of us are absolutely wrong, because in that very denial of worthiness, it's truly declared in our nature.

I love hanging out with service personnel of all branches and listening to their stories of lives before and after their service. In many cases it's clear the joining and deployment are demarcations in the flow of their tales.

Their lives were interrupted by war, by the burden they accepted in service of country and countrymen, and by the acts seen and conducted. For some, that interruption didn't stop when they got their separation papers, continuing through what the government allows in terms of reintegration processes. For so many of my friends, I'm pleased beyond words they were able to find solace in groups of like-minded men and women. It's amazing to watch them lift each other up.

I so proud we all hold that kind of determination and grace in our souls, granting a shoulder to lean on when asked, an ear to listen when there's distress, and a promise to always pick up.

Heroes come in all shapes and sizes—especially yours.

Woofully yours,
~ML

More Than Enough

When a man sees himself as damaged, imperfect, and flawed, it's hard to believe there could be love in his future. After a near-fatal accident stripped Blade of his confidence, he didn't hold out much hope ... for anything.

Until Jenn—gorgeous, sweet, and kind—dropped into his life.

Where he sees destruction, she sees perfection.

Where he sees helplessness, she sees courage.

Where he sees ruin, she sees strength.

Can he ever believe he's more than enough?

One

Blade

"Monk, hey Monk." Blade flinched at how his voice sounded, hating the neediness that coated each word out of his mouth these days.

Since the accident, it felt as if he was needy all the time, and he fucking hated it. Hated the holes in his memories that tripped him up, taking his composure as they exposed the flaws lodged in his brain. *Made it through three goddamned tours and a drunk bitch in a subcompact takes me out.*

Blade, known to his mom as Nathanael Murphy, waited as Monk finished talking to one of their newest scrubs, their prospects collectively called FNGs. Monk bounced a clenched fist off the top of the guy's shoulder a couple of times, then turned to Blade.

Alex Waterman, Monk, had stood beside Blade in the months since the accident, kicking his ass when appropriate, propping him up when that was needed. Blade didn't know what he'd have done without the man. *Prolly died*. If he wasn't honest with anyone else, he needed to be honest with himself. Taking a long walk had looked like a good option for a time, back when it was touch and go with the walking or the talking. Thank God Monk had seen and stepped in, or Blade wouldn't be here today to annoy him.

"Yo, Blade. How's it goin' today?"

Monk's hand reached out and captured Blade's, yanking him in for a one-armed clinch. Blade's head swam with the abrupt movement, and he swallowed hard, forcing the sick back into his belly.

After a long moment, his mouth agreed to cooperate. "You know, you know." Another pause, this one longer, but Monk waited patiently, keeping quiet. "Could be worse." He stepped back, pleased when he kept the tottering to a minimum. *Savin' face, one step at a time*. "Wondered if you, if you had a route planned for us yet."

Monk pursed his lips then grinned, nodding. "Yeah, we're gonna have a good run, brother. Got it all planned out."

Three goddamned tours.

The head injury suffered in the wreck last year continued to plague him through moments like this. Instants of time when the world dipped and swayed around him, puke rolling up his throat until it threatened to suffocate him and fearful thoughts working to drag him under. When his thoughts and mouth didn't align, words jumbled on their way off his tongue. The docs promised there were medications to help sort him out, but he fought through it, gutting it out again and again, until he hadn't the strength anymore. Repeatedly Monk had come to his rescue, unerringly finding him and talking him through the worst of it.

Those were the good endings to the bad days.

He'd had an equal number of bad-ending days, too.

Ass propped on the edge of the sagging couch cushion, Blade stared at the options laid in front of him on the low coffee table. Using the shaking of his hands like a dowsing rod, he stretched out his fingers, holding them over the different targets for long seconds, heartbeats of time that skipped madly away, never to be seen again.

Eenie… The bottle of pills the doc gave him along with a lecture about the strength and addictive nature of that particular medicine.

Meenie… His knee bumped the table, and the clear liquid sloshed lazily. Even through the closed container, he caught the acrid odor of moonshine.

Miney… Flat black, sleek, and made to fit his hand, the pistol rested on the cold surface, silently waiting.

*Mo… With a quick movement, he scooped up the motorcycle keys and pushed to his feet, swaying in place for a moment. Phone in hand, he strode outside, pausing only long enough to text an open invitation to the group chat that stayed at the top of his messages: **Taco Barn 10 min**.*

Blade hadn't been parked long when he heard the rumble of pipes in the distance. He looked up in time to see the trio approaching, neatly arranged in a stereotypical wedge formation as if they were still deployed and fighting. Monk in the lead, as usual, Neptune to his left, and Wolf to his right.

His brothers, determined to give Blade whatever he needed to keep an even keel.

That had been a good night.

"Where?" He pulled in a slow breath. "Where you takin' us, Monk?" He grinned up at the bigger man, antsy to start and get in the wind. That's where he'd been finding himself more and more, ranging far outside their normal territory at times. "Huh? Where?"

"Out and about, my brother. Out and about." Monk studied him, and Blade felt the weight of that regard, straightening his shoulders as if on the parade ground again. Chest out, chin lifted, he met Monk's gaze directly. "You good, Blade? How's the head, man?"

"Head's fine, fine. Real good these days." He fought off the need to look away, to lick his lips, to fidget in any way, knowing the smallest movement would reveal his true state of mind to Monk. Was it right to keep this from his road captain? Probably not, but Blade was already planning on asking for sweep, which would put him behind the pack and out of range, lessening the chance of fucking his brothers over with any instant of inattention. "Sweet. Life is sweet. Got my iron." He gestured to the side towards where his bike was parked. "My brothers." Arms sweeping out in a wide gesture, he indicated the world around them. "And the wind." Chin lifting even more, Blade let his eyes dip closed for an instant, blinking away the white spots cluttering his vision when he opened them again. "All, all, all a man like me needs."

Proving he could read Blade like a book, Monk shook his head and snorted a laugh. "Bitch, you're wanting to ride sweep, aren't you?"

Blade grinned, letting his shoulders sag the barest amount. "Yeah, brother. Gimme."

"Fucking hell, I'd like to actually ride with you one of these times, man." Someone called Monk's name from across the lot, and they both glanced that direction. A cluster of men were around a bike, and from the way one of them was gesticulating, there must be a problem with his ride. "Gotta deal with this." Monk dug in his pocket and pulled out a folded knife. Curling his fingers around the handle, he muttered, "Bet it's another slick. I need to make my rounds, man. I give you the high sign, can you open the shed?"

Blade nodded, rattling the keys in his pocket with a jingle. "Yeah, brother. We need to mount a tire, just let me, just let me know."

He didn't hold an official position within the club, but once Monk had started storing spare parts and tires in the outbuilding behind the clubhouse, Blade had quickly fallen into the role of wrench for the brothers who lacked the skills or inclination. He'd require they spend the time with him, patiently trying to pass along his knowledge earned both from growing up with a mechanic father and working on the tracks and Humvees while deployed overseas. Since Monk had become road captain, he took his duties seriously and did at least a visual inspection of every bike before rides. Wolf had friends on the racing circuit who'd been pleased to find a market for their take-offs, tires with too little tread to tackle hard turns on the track. Wolf proved to have connections with various wholesalers who'd been happy to start up a side business of motorcycle parts, cutting them a deal for a low percent markup. All of that meant Blade had what amounted to a full-time job now. Zero pay but filled to the brim with satisfaction.

"Brother." A light blow with a closed fist to his shoulder rocked him sideways. Wolf had walked up just as Monk stalked off, still-closed knife flipping back and forth between his fingers. "How's it hangin'?"

"Hard and low, man. Hard and low." Blade glanced at him from the corner of his eye and lifted his chin in greeting. "You ready to roll?"

"You know it. Born ready."

Neptune stepped up beside Wolf with a heavy sigh. "We ain't headin' out anytime soon, are we?"

They looked across the lot to where Monk crouched beside the bike, his neck twisted to look up at the owner with a scowl on his face.

Wolf let out a groan. "I'm thinkin' you're right. Fuck."

Blade listened to them with half his attention, the rest fixed on Monk. He grinned when his brother arrowed a glare across the lot towards him. Dipping his chin, he gave Monk a nod, then turned to Neptune and Wolf. "Work. I got work to do, my friends. I'll be quick, promise."

"Quick as you fuckin' can, brother. I'm ready to roll out. This shit's gettin' old." Neptune's tone held annoyance that Blade understood. "Problem with layerin' on new members is teachin' them what the fuck they're getting into."

"That's something you're well equipped to do, Sarge." It took a minute to get it out, but it was worth it to see Neptune's face just before the man scoffed at Blade's honorific for him. "And now, I'm gonna go do my thang."

Thirty minutes later, he grunted and yanked on the cheater bar as he finished tightening the final bolt fastening the back axle into place, tire replaced and drive belt adjustments complete. "We're good, Road Captain." Blade looked down, picking tools up from the piece of leather he'd thrown on top of the gravel. He was tired but wanted to keep reaching for more. Like the speech therapist told him, he wouldn't get better until he pushed behind where he was now. Slowly and steadily, he forced the words out. "Unless you've got some blinker fluid you need topped off." Wrenches and sockets in hand, he grinned up at Monk, who still wore a heavy scowl. "Brother." He handed the tools off to the bike owner. "Run put these up for me, would ya? I'll be there in a minute." Back on his feet, he dusted off his knees, then palm to palm, knocking loose the final bits of old, dried grease. "He's good, man. He wasn't thinkin' was all."

"Blowout at fifty woulda taken out everyone near him. Thinkin' needs to be the first thing these FNGs do." Monk blew out a lungful of air, scrubbing at the top of his head with a hand. "We'll be runnin' about an hour late now."

"Why's it matter? Why you in a hurry? You got an appointment or something?" Blade didn't miss Monk's flinch. For once his words came easily, the ability to rib Monk making him grin. "What the fuck? Wolf, you see this shit? Our boy's got himself a lil somethin' on tap, man. Gotchu a booty call later?" He shook his ass, doing the worst possible imitation of a twerk. "Booty call, booty call, booty booty booty call." That ended when Monk slugged his shoulder, not even pretending to pull the hit. "Mother*fucker*."

Then Wolf took up the taunt, and Monk launched himself at their brother, taking a bite to the ribs when he attempted to get the man into a headlock.

Blade laughed until he nearly pissed himself.

My brothers.

Two

Jenn

Leaning her shoulders against the outside wall of the diner, Jennifer Campbell flexed her toes inside shoes gone too tight, her feet cruelly swollen after only a few hours on them. She closed her eyes as the soft sounds of the surrounding forest thrummed through the air, cicadas humming in the trees a constant refrain. A slow breath in and Jenn thought of a faraway lake's shore, the waves a steady beat against the sand. She breathed out in time with that imagined wave, holding and waiting for the next incoming surge before she pulled in another breath. Slowly, she quieted her mind, the pain from her feet receding as surely as those waves did.

The sound of the cicadas changed, growing louder, deeper, rumbling until they shook the building behind her, and Jenn's eyes popped open, the imagined lake gone in a flash.

Not cicadas.

Motorcycles.

She whirled and hurried along the wall, turning into the back door of the kitchen just in time for Rose, the other waitress, to burst into the room. Face alight with excitement, Rose exclaimed, "There's a bunch of bikes just pulled in. Like sixty of them." Jenn met her gaze, and the two women smiled broadly. "Gonna be busy."

Jenn responded, "Those boys are good tippers, though. Worth the work."

"Amen, sister." Rose laughed and turned. "I'll prep glasses and coffee."

Jenn stepped up beside the line cook. "Want me to drop a couple baskets of fries?" He nodded distractedly, rapidly tossing burger and chicken patties onto the grill. "You got it." From the freezer to the deep fryer was only a couple of steps, and she'd just locked the second basket into the hot grease when Rose breezed back into the room.

"Filling up, gonna need you out front, Jenn." She tore a few sheets from her book, shoving the papers under the clips on the order wheel. "Boys are hungry."

She nodded and patted her apron pockets, verifying the presence of pen and her guest checkbook for taking orders. "Set."

Of the fourteen tables, all but two were occupied, each chair or bench seat taken. Glancing out the plate glass windows, she saw a mass of bikes still parking, leather vest-wearing men standing in clumps at various places on the lot. An older man claimed a stool at the counter just as she walked up, and he gave her a bright smile. There was a patch on his vest that proclaimed him president, and she thought it prudent to give him a gentle warning.

"We'll be full to overflowing with your crew. There're picnic tables outside for anyone who can't find a seat inside. Hope nobody minds." Empty coffee mug in hand, she angled her head and cocked an eyebrow at him, receiving a nod in response. "Burgers and fries are the fastest bet." Topping the mug to the rim, she shoved the coffee pot back onto the burner. "What'll you have?"

Blowing across the surface of the coffee, he sipped, smacked his lips, and verified he understood what she wasn't saying. "Burger and fries, doll. Sounds good."

"You got it." She jotted it down and leaned back into the kitchen to shove the order ticket onto the wheel.

Quickly making the rounds of the tables in her section, she set men up with water, sodas, and coffee, good-naturedly turning down a dozen gently inappropriate requests and collecting orders as she went. It wasn't until she hit the next-to-last table that things went awry. First, the two men had taken up a four-top, vests and helmets occupying the extra chairs at their table. That was just rude when more than a dozen men stood outside for lack of a table or seat. Then they hadn't even looked at the menus by the time she arrived at their table, hemming and hawing over the food choices as if this were a Michelin three-star establishment.

"No, I can come back." She held up a finger for the next table, four men who were watching with interest her failure to wrangle the two diners. "Take your time, make a choice."

She'd just turned away when she felt the touch on her butt. A gliding caress rather than a brutal grope, but unwelcome all the same. Jenn whirled and stared at the two men, who were grinning at her, daring her to say anything. She waffled for a moment then shook her head as she backed away, decision made. *Not worth it.*

One long step to the side put the final table between her and the two men. When she finished with those orders, she glanced back over to find the other two were still huddled over the menus, men from a nearby table now engaged, leaning close and offering suggestions. She could tell from the colorful pictures under the laminate that they'd moved away from the sandwich section and into the dinner entrees. *Great.*

By the time her orders were all turned in, her first plates were coming up, and she began the cycle all over again, this time whisking armfuls of hot food to the tables.

The two men were missing, belongings gone, seats now occupied by four new patrons who all ordered burgers and fries, waters to drink. Jenn sighed with relief and kept moving. To the kitchen, back to the dining room, back to the kitchen.

"Jenn, can you run outside to the storage shed? I need towels from out there." The cook was hustling in place, moving fast as he shook, flipped, slathered, and seasoned.

"Sure thing." She shoved against the crash bar with her butt, opening the door with a swivel of her hips. "Be right back."

The brilliant sunshine was a shock after the dimness of the diner, and it took a moment for Jenn's eyes to adjust.

That was a moment too long.

Three

Blade

"You know where the FNGs went?"

Wolf looked up at his question, brow furrowing as he chewed.

Blade glanced around the diner, verifying what he already knew. The two prospects that had been a pain in the ass earlier were no longer at their table. He twisted in his seat, scanning the bikes, focusing on the groups of men still outside. *Nada*.

"What's up, Blade?" Neptune's question made him whirl around, the world doing that damned dip and sway for a breath.

"I think the FNGs bailed on the run. I don't see their shit anywhere." Still on a roll with his words, he held to that warm feeling in his chest. It wasn't often he felt nearly normal. He shoved the last bite of his burger into his mouth and chewed, moved it to one side of his mouth, and said, "Gonna check outside, see if I find 'em." Scanning the table, he didn't see a ticket yet. "Y'all seen the waitress? I gotta pay." Wolf shook his head, so Blade sighed and pulled his wallet out. He tried to calculate the cost but gave up. Knowing it was ample money for the entire bill, he tossed three bills to the table and told them, "You owe me."

"Yeah, yeah." Wolf laughed. "So you say. I say you're volunteering to buy our lunch, asshole."

"Whatever." Blade gave him a single-finger salute and turned, leaving his brothers laughing behind him.

Outside, the heat pressed down on him, a welcome change from the wet and chill weather they'd suffered through lately. The cicadas were active, their humming roar rising and falling in volume as the breeze gusted through the trees. The diner was an unexpected gem, an island of parking and building surrounded on three sides by forest, fronted by a well-maintained highway. Another example of why Monk was the perfect choice for the club's road captain. He'd found the place and then planned a ride, organizing the event so this place became their meal stop.

A brief sound interrupted the cicadas, and Blade jerked around, staring into the woods. Listening intently, he heard it again and realized the acoustics of the clearing were bending the sound back around to him, but the origin wasn't off in the woods. It was around the corner of the building.

Two strides took him to the edge, and he turned that corner to see nothing. Curious, because that sound had been somehow desperate, he walked the length of wall and rounded the corner, slapping a smile in place to defuse whatever he might be walking into. Blade rocked back on a heel, head jerking back in shock.

The prospects, those FNGs, had the waitress trapped against the wall. They weren't touching her, not yet, but from the aggressive way they crowded in on either side, it was only a matter of time.

"Hey, hey," he barked out the words, following with a command. "Get, get, get." Rage boiled through him at how his body failed at this critical moment. "Get the fuck away from her."

The two men, and fuck him if he could remember their names, stared at him—and one, the taller, the one he remembered from the last clubhouse party as being a mean drunk, licked his fucking lips and shook his head.

"We saw her first."

"The fuck you mean? This isn't a, a game, a game of dibs, mother*fucker*." He dropped intentional pauses between his words, one of the techniques the therapist had recommended. "Get. The fuck. Away from her." She was pressed back against the wall, head turned to the side, and he saw what looked like the outline of a hand on her neck. That was the last straw, the one that tipped him over into warrior mode, all hesitation put aside in his certainty that she needed protecting. That *he* needed to protect *her*.

Blade stepped close and straight-armed a blow from the heel of his hand into the throat of the taller man. He ignored the choking sounds and kicked sideways, catching the man's knee with the heel of his boot, taking him to the ground with a sweep of his foot. Blade pushed between the woman and the remaining FNG, powerfully shoving the man in the chest so he stumbled backwards and tripped, landing on his ass in the gravel. Blade was on him in a moment, fist rising and falling until the man stopped fighting back.

It was the work of moments to strip their prospect vests from them, and Blade didn't give a fuck he wasn't an officer and didn't really have the authority to make that decision. "This is mine. My club," he growled as he yanked the blue jean fabric down the men's arms. "And you're. Fouling it. With your shit. You'll never, never be. A member. I'll see to it."

With a final disgusted glare at the two men attempting to move away, Blade dismissed them and turned his back, the ultimate insult in his mind, meaning they weren't worth his time or concern. The waitress stood still, her gaze fixed on him, whites of her eyes revealing the terror still coursing through her system. Blade lifted a hand, inordinately pleased when she didn't flinch from his touch, gentle against the ill-used column of her neck.

"Are you okay?" Blade curled his lips at the inane question. "I mean, of course. Of course you aren't okay. Not after that." He leaned closer and caught the scent of her perfume, light and summery, and it left him unexpectedly wanting to experience more of her. "Did they hurt you?"

"No." The wince when she swallowed put the lie to her statement. "I'm okay." Her eyes dipped closed, lines of her face deepening as she fought with something. "Your timing was impeccable. I don't think they would have taken it much further, but I'm glad you helped put a stop to it." Lashes quivering against the swell of her cheek, the waitress—he caught sight of her nametag and tried the word out mentally: *Jenn*—lost the fight for a moment, a single tear escaping to trail a wet track down her face. "Thank you."

The muscles of her throat moved under his hand, making Blade aware he still touched her. Instead of dropping his hold, he curled his fingers around the back of her neck and swayed the tiniest bit closer. "You sure? You're not hurt?"

Jenn's eyes flashed open, and he sucked in a breath when he saw the wide, dark circles of her pupils. Aroused, not frightened. Not anymore.

Staring into her eyes, Blade felt an inexorable pull he knew he needed to fight. She'd just been traumatized, had suffered through being intimidated by men who hadn't been as far into her personal space as he was already. He wet his lips, and his heart skipped a beat when her gaze dropped to his mouth, her tongue coming out and sweeping a matching stripe along her bottom lip.

Gravel crunched along the side of the building, and he blinked, breaking free from the spell holding him captive. Jenn's lashes fluttered and she arched towards him as Blade stepped backwards, putting distance between them. Another slow blink and he watched as barriers fell into place, Jenn walling herself off from him, making Blade immediately miss the surprising tenderness of the previous moments.

"Yeah." She breathed the word, and he cocked his head, confused. "I'm sure. I'm okay." She shook her head, straightening and stepping sideways, adding more space to what he'd already given. "Like I said, thanks for your help." Another sideways step. "I need to get back inside." Her gaze darted past him, and fear crawled across her features. He turned to see Wolf and Neptune walking towards them. "Thanks for stopping by."

She was at the door, fingers wrapped around the handle, by the time he turned back to her. He realized that in another moment she'd be gone, and no matter if he raced around and met her inside, it wouldn't be the same. "Jenn." On impulse, he called her name and waited. Body stiff, she angled her head to look at him. "I'm Blade." *And you're way out of my league.*

Gazes locked together, they stood like that for a breath. Then she nodded, and he saw her lips move, mouthing the sounds of his name.

Blade.

Four

Jenn

Inside the kitchen, surrounded by the familiar smells and rushing energy of orders being prepared, Jenn took a moment to slump back against the door, pulling in a long, slow breath. Eyes closed, she tried to focus on the lakeshore in her mind, giving it up as a failed attempt only seconds into the exercise.

She jolted when a hand landed on her arm. Twisting away with a cry, Jenn opened her eyes to find Rose standing in front of her, a frightened expression on her face.

"Jenn? What happened?"

Pulling herself together, she took in a deep breath and gave Rose a brusque headshake. "I'm okay. Couple of guys approached me outside, but it's nothing."

"You sure?"

With a laugh, she nodded. "Sure, I'm sure. Sorry about disappearing on you like that. Took a minute to shake free of them." Dusting her palms together, she found them covered with grit from being pressed against the outside wall. She stepped to the utility sink and scrubbed her hands briskly, asking over her shoulder, "Need me to cover any of your tables?"

"No, they're almost done." Rose hesitated, then asked again, "Are you really sure?"

"Yeah. I'm good." She grabbed the last of the paper towels off the roll to dry her hands, only then recalling what she'd gone outside for. Deep in her belly, her stomach did a sickening flip and roll, the remembered fear as the two men had boxed her in threatening to swallow her for an instant.

The sound levels rose in the dining room; men were shouting, their voices sounding angry. Chair legs scraped the floor, sounding like a wild herd of buffalo stampeding towards the kitchen.

"What now?" Jenn turned to the swinging door, feeling Rose crowd in behind her.

The older man she'd served earlier walked through, stiff-arming the door so it swung wide; behind him were two men. Disappointment threaded through her when she saw neither of them was Blade. The grizzled look shading the man's beard and hair didn't lessen the impact of how angry he was, and Jenn stiffened her spine as he strode directly to her, stopping nearly toe-to-toe, black biker boots next to her sensible rubber-soled shoes.

"Are you okay?" The question wasn't quiet, and she could feel the anger rolling off him in waves. Jenn nodded, but he shook his head, chin dipping until he stared directly into her eyes. "Put words to it, darlin'."

Jenn struggled to speak, her throat closing tight as tears sprang to life in her eyes.

He studied her for a moment, then whirled a stride away, roaring, *Fuck.*" As fast as he'd turned from her, he spun back, crowding closer with a shouted, "Are you fuckin' okay?"

A familiar frame appeared in front of her and Jenn took a step back, unsurprised when Blade matched the movement, staying close to her. He'd shoved himself between the president and Jenn. Leaning forwards, he yelled, those same odd pauses between his words, "Back. The fuck. Off. You're scaring, scaring her worse, man."

Then, just as he had outside, he turned his back on the man, his worried eyes studying her intently. Close enough to feel his breath, she didn't startle when he gripped her wrist, pulling her even closer.

"Jenn." That flip and roll was back in her belly, but it wasn't fear this time. She hadn't feared him earlier, either, her gut telling her this man was honorable and trustworthy. "You're safe. Okay? You know that, right? You're safe."

"Yeah." Her voice came out softer than she wanted, trembling to match the rest of her. Blade's hand tightened around her wrist, and she gently twisted free from his grip. The sadness in his eyes only lasted a moment before Jenn placed both hands against his chest. "I'm okay." She tried for a laugh, only partly successful. "Again."

Slowly, as if afraid she'd protest, Blade rested his hands on either side of her waist. His fingers tangled in her apron strings when she smiled up at him.

"Those two. They aren't part, part of our club. They weren't yet, and now won't. They won't ever be." Blade shifted to the side and indicated the president with a tip of his head. "Gibby won't stand for that kind of asshole wearin' his colors."

"Blade." At her use of his name, Blade's eyes widened, and his hands jerked her a little closer. "I'm okay, really. Nothing bad happened."

"Could have." Gibby stepped into her line of sight. "I'm glad it didn't." Two men backed through the swinging doors into the kitchen, and Jenn looked to see each carried full tubs of dirty dishes. She turned to Blade with a question, but before she opened her mouth, Gibby answered. "I can't stop it from happening, that's already behind us. But I can make life easier for you." He gestured towards the two now piling dishes into the sink. "Come out front with Blade, sit a spell and get to know us. The real us." Arms spread wide, Gibby smiled, teeth flashing white in his beard. "We are the Borderline Freaks, and we're gonna be in your corner always. Welcome to the family, Jenn."

She watched silently as he turned and walked out, and except for Blade, the other club members followed him. Jenn blinked. "What just happened?"

Rose laughed, the cook scrambled to keep things from burning, and Blade stared at her, gaze unwavering as he said, "You just got adopted. By a motorcycle club president."

Oh, Lord.

Five

Blade

He sat his bike on a corner of the lot, studying the empty expanse of gravel in front of him.

A quick conversation with Monk had secured another sweep assigned for the remainder of the run, the man's expression unreadable as Blade told him he'd be hanging here. Unspoken was the reason: to ensure the two FNGs now cut from the club didn't return to hassle Jenn.

Gibby had agreed with him, wordlessly clapping Blade on the shoulder as he strode past to his own bike, rolling out of the lot in his privileged position behind Monk. Gibby was a good man, fair and always aware of the public perception of his club. When Blade approached him with repossessed vests in hand and the story of what had happened, Gibby's expression hadn't taken long to grow stony and angry.

Him racin' into the kitchen took me off guard. Blade snorted as he remembered the surprise in the old man's eyes when Blade jumped in and set him back on his heels. That took him to remembering the look of sweet trust on Jenn's face when he'd turned to face her, and the heat in his chest returned twofold.

The kitchen door opening caught at his attention, and he watched as Jenn and the other waitress walked out, heads bent together as they laughed at something. Jenn stopped in her tracks and stared when she noticed him. Rose said something he didn't catch, and Jenn responded, "No, it's okay. You go on home. See you tomorrow."

Then, shoulders back, she stalked towards him. Or attempted to, anyway, but her gingerly placed steps lent her a far less imposing presence. Blade grinned, then tried to wipe it from his face, dipping his chin to hide the expression when he was unsuccessful.

"What are you doing still here?" She stopped just out of reach, a move he mourned. "I thought you left a while ago."

"I'm just sittin'." He shrugged and rested his wrist on the handlebar. "Just hangin' out."

Jenn rolled her eyes. "Liar. You're watching out for me."

"Maybe," he allowed with a smile.

"Again." She stepped closer and placed her hand on the grip next to his, so close he felt the heat from her fingers. "You've done enough, Blade."

Fuck. He liked hearing his name on her lips. Soft and slow, like her mouth didn't want to let the sounds go, like she wanted to hold him in her mouth awhile. And that idea started a party in his pants, his dick chubbing up more than a little.

He shifted on the bike's seat. "Just makin' sure you're okay." She smiled when he admitted the truth, and the beauty in that tiny quirk of her lips was mind-blowing. "Damn, you're pretty."

That earned him a wider grin, and she rolled her eyes again as she muttered dismissively, "Shut up."

Blade watched her for a moment, unsure what his heart was telling him. She was stunning, with her thick, dark hair pulled back into a ponytail, warm brown eyes looking steadily at him. "You headed home?" She nodded. "Go on then." He pointed his chin at the only car left on the lot. "You've gotta be tired. Been on your feet all day."

"Okay." She didn't move right away, just kept looking at him with that smile curling her generous mouth. Huffing out a sigh, she took a step back. "Okay. Ride safely, Blade."

"Yes, ma'am." He dipped his chin to his throat, holding her stare until he watched her turn and start to walk away. "I'll see you around, Jenn."

Six

Jenn

Jenn leaned her forehead against the steering wheel, twisting the key in the ignition again and listening to the tiny clicks sounding from underneath the hood. She sighed and lifted her head, looking at the empty parking lot behind the diner. It was her first closing shift since the unsettling events a couple of weeks ago and the first time she remembered being alone since then. Normally she liked working Sundays, because the diner closed after a late lunch, which left her the entire evening for herself.

"Of course you'd pick this moment to die." Rose and Greg, the new line cook, had just driven away after locking the building behind them. "No other time would do, right?"

She shoved the door open, stepping out of the hot car into the only slightly less inferno-level of the unshaded gravel parking lot. Leaning back in, she pulled the lever to pop the hood before slamming the door hard enough to rock the vehicle on its springs.

Hood propped up, she stared at the engine for a moment, wracking her brain for memories of what her father would do in this situation. Tentatively at first, she reached for the cables leading away from the battery, wrinkling her nose at the crusted grease and corrosion on the ends. She checked each, finding them firmly attached. "Okay, so it's not a loose cable." Chewing her bottom lip, she glared at the engine. "And that's the extent of my knowledge."

Resigning herself to the fact she'd have to call for help, she bent into the car, sweeping the interior for her purse and not seeing it. "What the...?" She looked around again, seeing the same drift of trash behind the front seat, a lightweight sweater draped over the passenger seat, her rolled apron on the console—and no purse anywhere to be seen.

Straightening, she stared at the diner as she ran her vague memories of the last few minutes through her mind. "No." Joking with Rose, watching Greg shyly flirting with her co-worker, Jenn had walked out of the building with keys in hand, her purse left sitting on the edge of the opened locker shelf. "Oh, no."

A glance around the parking lot told her what she already knew. Hers was the last vehicle present. The diner didn't open again until tomorrow morning, and there was no remnant of a past era in the form of an old-fashioned payphone. The diner sat in the middle of a swath of privately owned forest, on a lightly trafficked local highway.

As if to prove her wrong, she heard an engine rapidly approaching, but before she could even take a half a dozen steps, the truck had whizzed into and out of view, the sound dwindling in the distance.

"Okay." She sighed. "Clearly, little traffic doesn't mean no traffic." It was fifteen miles to town, and another three to her rented house. Walking at three miles an hour, that would take her… "Six hours. Ugh."

She left the hood up, propped a note on the dash to explain where she was going, and peeled the largest bills from her roll of tips. Folding them into a compact bundle, she stared down at her waitress uniform with a frown. No pockets. With an eye roll, she tucked the money and her keys into her bra, wedging them into her limited cleavage, leaving the rest of it and her heat-trapping apron behind.

It was hot on the road, the sound of the cicadas a continual roar as the trees closed in, providing splotchy shading for the highway. An hour into her walk, there had still been no cars driving past, which wasn't surprising for a lazy Sunday. Still, she'd hoped to have gotten a ride by that point. Belatedly she thought about the two men who'd pinned her against the back wall of the diner two weeks earlier. With a shiver, she suddenly regretted not bringing even an improvised weapon with her. While the odds of a serial killer stopping to pick her up were slim to none, there still had to be a chance of some kind. Jenn cast a glance towards the trees, seeing only a few small sticks lying on the forest floor. *Dammit.*

To her pleasure and chagrin, no trash dotted the ditches, either. She walked another half an hour without seeing a cast-off bottle or anything else she could have used to defend herself. Anxious and tense, she kept circling back to her memories of that day at the diner no matter how she tried to keep them out.

She honestly hadn't worried about the two men until she'd seen Blade waiting at the end of her shift. The fact he'd stayed behind while his friends rode on had spoken volumes, and Jenn had kept her guard up for several days until it was clear that the two jerks weren't going to come back for a repeat.

While the harassment had been terrifying when it happened, with her not certain how far the two men were willing to push things, Jenn sighed as she remembered the moment Blade had come to her rescue. His broad back had appeared in front of her as if by magic, and she'd dreamed about his fluid movements as he fought off the men, defending her. Then the tender way he'd treated her afterwards, cautious and caring. She'd felt cherished, which wasn't a feeling she'd ever gotten even from a boyfriend. But Blade, the stranger who saved her, made her feel good.

"Stop it." Her muttered words surprised her, a discordant contrast to the rise and fall of the breeze and insects. Nothing came out of romanticizing those moments. He'd found a woman forced into what could have easily become a full-on attack, stood up for her, then made certain she wasn't injured or frightened too badly. He'd have done the same for Rose if she'd been the unlucky one. *But it wasn't Rose. It was me.*

She shook the thought away, trudging onwards, one foot in front of the other, minutes ticking past as she walked into the deepening shadows between the trees.

Seven

Blade

He'd already rolled past the diner before he realized the car with the raised hood was Jenn's. Slowing, he put a boot down and made a U-turn in the middle of the road, not having to wait on traffic. He'd been riding this road every night for the past two weeks and had marked the limited traffic once the sun started setting.

With his bike parked next to Jenn's car, he dismounted and glanced under the hood, then leaned close to read a handwritten note stuffed on the dash. **Car won't start, walking home.**

Blade glanced around the diner, knowing they'd closed nearly three hours ago. He hadn't passed her walking so far, which meant if he continued on his route, he'd probably stumble upon her somewhere closer to town.

Unless some jackhole picked her up first.

Blade scowled and strode to the bike, the engine turning over on the first try, roaring underneath him.

Unless some drunk bitch plowed through her, leaving her dead in the ditch.

The sweat that prickled the back of his neck had nothing to do with the heat.

After not having the dreams for weeks, months even, these past few nights had been a spectacular sleeping fail, waking up with a shout just as the dream drunk smashed into his bike, throwing Blade high into the air, arms and legs pinwheeling in a ragdoll dance of pain. Even knowing that wasn't how it'd happened wasn't enough to derail the vicious circle of his imagination. He had no real memories of the accident but had gone over the police report and photos enough to recognize that the truth of what happened wasn't what his mind twisted it into. Didn't matter when his sleep was a shitshow.

Blade swallowed hard and steadied the bike as he roared out of the parking lot, rolling the throttle to gun the engine, racing along the highway, chasing the last of the light.

There'd been nothing for miles until, rounding a curve, he caught sight of a figure standing in the oncoming lane, arms waving overhead. Toe to the shifter, he worked his way down through the gears in rapid descent, coming to a full stop only feet away from Jenn. She'd bent over, hands on her knees as she sucked in air, looking exhausted. She muttered, "Oh, thank God."

Off the bike, he paused only long enough to retrieve a bottle filled with water from the holder he'd bolted to the frame, then stooped next to her. "Hey." Her head jerked up at his roughened voice, and he saw tears in her eyes. "Oh, hey, no. You're okay, promise." Kneeling on the gritty highway surface, he reached out and cupped her cheek. Her skin was hot to the touch, and he realized she was overheated from the exertion in the broiling summer evening, probably without knowing it. "Here, Jenn. Drink a little."

She accepted the bottle from him with shaking hands, but then couldn't unfasten the top. Wordlessly, she held it back out to him with a plea in her eyes. He opened it and watched as she carefully took a long drink. "Slow. Just a little at a time." She nodded, the bottle propped against her chin, her breathing gradually evening out. "How long have you been walking?"

"Since mid-afternoon?" Rough and crackling, her voice betrayed her emotions, and he stood to thread a supporting arm around her waist, pulling her tight against him. She came without argument and, cheek pressed to his chest, lifted the bottle and took another drink. "I'm tired, Blade."

"I bet you are. Car conked out on you, huh?" She nodded. "Want a lift home?" She sighed and wiggled around until she could eye his bike. *That's not a yes.* "Ever ridden a bike?"

"No." She wilted against him. "First time for everything."

"That's the spirit. I'll keep you safe. Take you home. Get you settled." It was quiet, the only sounds a faraway rumble of a river battling against the constant drone of insects. "Come on. Let's get going. Sooner we get you out of the heat, the better."

She didn't argue when he retrieved the bottle, and her eyes stayed fixed on him, watching everything he did. "Okay."

Staring at the bike for a moment, his stomach clenched when he realized he just had the one helmet. Since the accident, he hadn't ridden a single mile without one, knowing that another TBI could be bad news for him. It had been only pure luck he'd been wearing one the day he got hit, coming back from a memorial ride. He knew what he needed to do, because as nauseating as the idea of riding without a helmet was, the image of Jenn without one was crippling. It took him three attempts to get his mouth to cooperate, but he finally choked out the words. "I want you to wear this." He picked the helmet up off the seat and turned it around in his hands, staring into the shadows inside. With a deep breath, he turned and held it out to her. "It'll be a little big, but better than nothing."

"What about you?" She took it and looked down as she fumbled with the clip, shoulders slumped as she fought to adjust the chinstrap. Finally, as she had with the bottle, she held it out to him. "I'm sorry."

"Don't worry about it." He evaluated her as he changed the setup for her smaller head. "You're dehydrated and overheated. And exhausted on top of that. I just want to get you home."

Chin up, she closed her eyes as she gave him access to secure the helmet. The backs of his fingers grazed the smooth skin of her throat, and Blade wanted to create a reason to touch her again.

She wiggled her jaw, testing the tightness of the strap before opening her eyes and smiling at him. "I live just past the old granary. There's a little cottage off on the right. That's me."

He nodded, picturing it in his mind as he mounted the bike. With exaggerated movements, she climbed on behind him, feet to the pegs and her hands on his shoulders. Blade leaned back as he started the bike, speaking over the rumble of the pipes, "I'll go slow, but hold on to my waist. Tight."

Her grip shifted, and he looked down to see her hands overlapping on his stomach. She'd curled the fingers of one hand around her other wrist, taking him at his word. Blade took off gently, letting her feel the slight jerk of the bike as he shifted gears. Sooner than he liked, they were through town and he saw what had to be her driveway in the distance, darkened silos and buildings of the granary flashing past. The lane was long and winding, dirt and rocks for the most part, but Jenn was game and held tight the whole way.

He pulled up in front of the cottage and killed the bike, waiting for her to step off the pegs. She didn't move, leaning heavily against his back. Blade glanced over his shoulder to see her eyes closed.

"Jenn?"

"Home, yay." Her voice was roughened again, dry and rasping. "Gimme a minute." He chuckled, and she tipped her head up, one eye opening slightly. "You're warm."

"And you got too hot. Come on. Let's get inside." He separated her hands, pulling her grip free from where she held his shirt.

She sounded slightly drunk, and he was alarmed to realize her words were slurring the least bit. "Okay, okay."

"Come on." Off the bike, he turned and removed the helmet, shocked to find her hair soaked but her skin hot and dry. Hanging the helmet from the handlebars by the strap, he scooped her up in his arms and stalked to the front door, ignoring her protests. It was locked, and he looked down at her. "Where's the key?"

"In my boobs." She lifted her head from where it rested against his chest. "Back door's not locked, though. You'd be safe from boob keys."

"Jesus," he muttered, whirling and jumping the short distance from the porch to the ground. Around the back of the house, he found her words true. The door opened easily, letting them into the kitchen. He knew what he needed, and fortunately the house appeared to follow a standard layout, so he turned right, angled into a narrow hallway, and proceeded until he found her bedroom. Two doors off the room told him she had an attached bath, which was a blessing right about now.

Blade set her on the edge of the bed, kneeling at her feet to unlace and remove her shoes. "Got anything in your pockets you don't want getting wet?" He gave a silent prayer of thanks for the way his mouth was cooperating right now.

She stared at him. He rose and opened the first door, revealing the bathroom. Stepping in, he started the shower on a lukewarm setting, then plugged the tub to collect the running water. Once again standing over her, he frowned at the puzzled look on her face as he toed out of his boots and took off his vest.

"Jenn, anything you don't want getting wet?"

"No pockets," she said, lifting a hand to fish in her bra for an instant, revealing smooth mounds of creamy flesh that made his mouth water. "See?" Palm up, she showed him what she'd retrieved, and he laughed. Keys and a small wad of cash.

"No phone?" Belt and wallet followed the vest to rest on top of her dresser, key fob and phone next. He patted his pockets to verify he hadn't forgotten anything important.

"In my purse, in the diner. That's why I couldn't call for a ride." In the chill of the air-conditioned house, she was beginning to sound slightly more lucid, and that was a good sign.

"Alrighty." He scooped her up again, paying no more attention to her demands to be put down than he had before. Once in the bathroom, he deposited her under the spray from the shower, climbing in behind her and holding her in place.

"Blade." Her yell was shrill while still managing to be rough. "Stop it."

"Nope. Gotta cool you down. I'm pretty sure you're riding the edge of heatstroke, Jenn. Stay with me." She lashed out, catching him in the side with her fist. "Ow. Stop it." He captured her wrists in one hand, holding firm as she twisted, trying to get away. "Jenn." She wasn't paying attention to him—and also wasn't staying under the shower like he wanted—so he whirled them and trapped her arms between their bodies as he held her tight to his front. "Shhhh, honey."

Shuffling them around until she was positioned under the stream of water, he held her until the rising level in the tub had climbed halfway to their knees. By then she'd stopped struggling, relaxing against him without another complaint as the water began to do its work. He bent to the side and turned off the shower portion, then made it to his ass without too much splashing, Jenn between his legs, cradled to his chest. Turning off the warm water, he let the stream of cold run for a few minutes, chilling the nearly full tub. The silence when he cut the cold was profound, weighty. Even on this side of town, there wasn't much traffic, most folks traveling through doing so on the north-south route instead of east-west. Her house was far enough off the little highway Blade wasn't sure he'd hear any cars passing by anyway. It felt like he'd entered a soothing cocoon of peace and quiet.

"How you feelin' now?" He tried to gauge the time they'd been in the bathroom, but that was a sense that'd abandoned him after the accident, full days passing sometimes before he realized.

"Better." She shifted and he relaxed his hold, surprised when she snuggled in closer, head on his shoulder. "A lot better. I didn't realize what was happening."

"Yeah, sneaks up on ya." He lay there, listening to tiny ripples of water lapping against the side of the tub and the sound of her breathing, slow and deep.

The roar from his stomach was loud and unexpected. So was the bright music of her giggle afterwards.

"Yeah, I didn't have supper yet." Blade chuckled, and Jenn giggled louder. "So sue me. I had more important things to worry about."

"I could eat." Jenn's whisper was quiet, stilling his humor immediately. "Let me feed you, Blade. I'd be honored."

"You don't have to." It was a half-assed protest, and he knew it. So did she if the tiny giggle was anything to measure by. "But if you're offering, I'm accepting."

With the water draining, exiting the tub proved more difficult than entering it had been, his soaked socks having no grip on the slippery bottom. After a particularly close call, he realized a laughing Jenn was holding him up instead of the other way around. Glancing down, he found her looking up at him, the smile and warmth in her expression his alone. *All mine.* He froze at the thought, and by the time he'd decided to kiss her, the moment was over and she'd pulled away, grabbing towels from the cabinet.

She laid them on the counter, then retrieved a couple more. "I've got some things that should mostly fit you. I'll get changed, then grab them so you don't have to schlep around in your wet things." Towels pressed to her breasts, she paused. "Thank you, Blade." A brief smile played across her lips. "Again. Seems I'm always thanking you." Her chin ducked as she turned to the door.

"My pleasure," he said, but too late as the door closed behind her, shutting him in and her out.

Eight

Jenn

Wet clothes in a basket, waiting for Blade's to join them so she could wash and dry them, Jenn leaned against the counter, head bowed. She still had a pounding headache, but at least it had eased after she'd drained a bottle of water. She had the fixings for sandwiches arranged on a platter, just needed to assemble them for her guest.

Stupid.

She'd known she was getting hot but had been too far away from the diner when the idea of water crossed her mind, and even darting into the forest every so often hadn't brought much relief from the relentless heat. Thank goodness Blade had come along when he had, or she could be lying alongside the highway somewhere.

She hadn't been making good decisions by then, as evidenced by her embarrassing behavior. At least Blade had recognized the signs and taken steps to help cool her down. As shaky as she felt now, she knew it was a near-miss encounter.

"Hey. Hey, Jenn." The quiet greeting was paired with a soft touch on her hip, and Jenn lifted her head to see Blade had come up behind her, his bare feet silent on the tile floor. He had his wet things bundled under his arm. "How ya feelin' now?"

"I'll be fine." She reached out, and they had an annoying but hilarious tiny tug-of-war over the wet things before she huffed out a breath, giving up. "Put them there." She pointed at the basket. "I'll get them into the washer." He glanced over, then back to her with a shake of his head. "What? Are you going to ride home like that?" She gestured to his bare torso and feet, the too-large sweat pants hanging dangerously low off his narrow hips.

"Where's the washer?" He turned in a comical half circle before walking towards the basket, dumping his clothes on top of hers before picking it up. "Never mind. Found it." Blade disappeared into the tiny laundry room off the back of the kitchen. Then his head popped back out, gaze pinning her in place. "Your stuff need anything special?" He raked his fingers through his hair as she shook her head.

"Okay then, sit your ass down before you fall down, Jenn. I'm right here."

"You're doing the laundry?"

Out of sight, he laughed from his position next to the washing machine. "Yeah, that's one of the many things Uncle Sam made sure I knew how to do." The machine's controls clicked, followed by a gush of water. Then the thud of the lid closing preceded his reentrance into the kitchen. "Woman, do you ever do anything you're told?" Blade slipped an arm around her back before steering her to a chair he pulled out from under the kitchen table. "Sit down, Jenn. Let's get you fed."

Stunned by his forceful persistence, she sat, his hand gliding in a gentle touch along her shoulders as he turned away. An empty plate appeared, then a glass filled to the rim with ice and water.

She looked up and found him staring down at her, tongue caught in the corner of his mouth as if he were studying hard. "What?" It was tough to wrap her head around how comfortable he seemed, moving from one logical task to the next without prompting, as if couplehood were a long-established thing for them.

"I'm pegging you as a ham and tomato gal, on wheat with mayo." He turned away, treating her to the sight of his broad back once again, but this a more unique view. He had the classic physique of a swimmer with wide shoulders, bare skin browned from the sun, muscles playing under the smooth skin as he moved things on the countertop. He twisted to glance at her, the position showing off how his chest was as impressive as his back. All of that was topped by a handsome face with an expressive mouth and soulful eyes that didn't hide his feelings. He had proven to be an open book, for her at least, but maybe he was doing that on purpose to put her at ease.

The chair beside her moved and another plate appeared, this one loaded with three sandwiches. The chair shifted again as a bag of chips was placed in the center of the table, and then a final time as Blade sat, beer in hand. He was close enough his thigh brushed hers with every move, heat from his body baking into her. Unlike the dangerous reaction to being outside in the hottest portion of the day, this filled her chest with a gently simmering wave. Other than her landlord, the only men who'd been in the house were her brother and one of his friends, and the two of them had been more grunt-and-point guys than ones to hold a conversation. The contrast between the men was stark. By the way butterflies occupied her stomach around Blade, she found everything about him not just welcome, but most intriguing.

She watched as he transferred one sandwich to her plate, then reached out and dragged the chips closer. "There you go." He twisted in his chair, his leg rubbing against hers in an innocent touch. "You got a nice place."

"Thanks." Jenn lifted her glass, having to quickly use both hands to hide the trembling as she sipped. "Is this a thing you do?" Without looking at him, she retrieved half of the sandwich he'd made for her and took a bite, sinking her teeth into sun-ripened tomato sliced the perfect thickness and topped with sweet, smoked ham. He didn't answer, so she finished chewing and asked again. "Is it? This rescuing thing your gig?"

"Rescuing gig?" He scoffed around a mouthful of sandwich, his looking like a roast beef, piled with pickles. "Nope. I work construction. Rescuing women is my side hustle." He tipped his head and grinned at her, winking as he lifted the beer and took a deep drink. "You look better."

"This?" She liked the light feel of the conversation and teasingly tossed her head, still-wet hair trailing down her back. "Trust me, I can put together something infinitely better than the post-being-fried-in-the-sun look I've got going for me now."

"Meh." He shrugged. "You look good, Jenn. Every time I've met you, I've seen a little more." She glanced down at her tank top, and he sputtered into his beer. "No. God, no. I didn't mean that. I didn't, I mean."

"Relax, big guy. I'm joking." Jenn leaned close and bumped his shoulder with hers. "But you're right. In fact, I'm definitely seeing a lot more of you now than before." He stared at her again, the expression on his face inscrutable for the first time. Intent, piercing, it was hard to meet head on, but she held his gaze as best she could. "And I don't mind what I've seen of you so far, Blade. You're a genuinely good man."

"Nathanael." He looked startled, then smiled ruefully as he shook his head. "Nate Murphy." Sketching a short bow from his seat, he held his palm out and waited until she reached to grip it, shaking her hand up and down twice. "Pleased to meet you."

"Jennifer Campbell." She gave his fingers a squeeze. "My friends call me Jenn."

"Well, since I've already been doing that, I guess you'll have to let me into your friend circle. Foregone conclusion." Blade picked up his sandwich and gave it a scowl as he poked sliding pickles back into place. "Jenn."

"Nate." She responded in kind as she lifted half her sandwich and took a bite.

"Who's the boyfriend?"

She choked and coughed, his hand giving her a couple of solid thumps between her shoulder blades. "What?" She recovered, and he turned away. Head down, he didn't look at her as he bit into his sandwich. He hadn't answered her reflexive question either, but she knew she'd heard him correctly. "Boyfriend?"

Blade nodded, shoving approximately half the sandwich into his mouth at once. He still wasn't looking at her, which gave her a chance to study him. Ruddy color had crept up his neck and into his cheeks, and she had a feeling the blurted question mattered more than he'd wanted to give away.

"I don't have a boyfriend." His head jerked slightly, eyes glancing in her direction before zeroing back in on his plate. "No boyfriend, no manfriend, no husband or significant other. I mean—" She gestured around the kitchen at the curtains and decorative kitchen towels hanging from the drawer handles. "You think a man would want to live in this ruffled paradise?"

The corner of his mouth curved up as he shook his head side to side.

"Why did you think I had a boyfriend?"

Blade gestured down his body, and she struggled to not let her gaze get stuck on his chest and abs, defined pecs and six-pack on full display.

"I don't know what that means, Blade."

"Sweats. These aren't yours, woman." He plucked at the waistband, the tug on the elastic creating a delicious shadow on his belly, exposing a tiny trail of hair leading down. "If they aren't yours, then, with a woman like you, boyfriend is the next logical choice."

"Woman like me?" She turned sideways in her chair, elbow on the table. "What does that mean?"

He gestured vaguely towards her, the color in his cheeks deepening. "You know."

"No, I don't. What did you mean?" Now Jenn was intrigued. She had an idea, because he'd made it clear he reacted to her physically, but at this point, she wanted to see if she could make him admit it. "Tell me, Blade. What is a woman like me?"

"Jesus, you always talk everything to death?" Another enormous bite of his sandwich was sliced off by an aggressive bite, and she watched him chew. "What?" Muttering through the food, he didn't sound like he was willing to give on this.

"It's a weekend evening. Don't you have better things to do than rescue me?" She gestured towards him, using the same vague motion he had. "You know, a man like you?"

"The fuck's that mean?" Only after the words had burst from him did Blade seem to realize what he'd done, and he hung his head, shooting her a sheepish look. "Okay. *Fuck.* I just meant how pretty you are. No way on this green earth you're available."

"Are you asking me, or telling me?" Jenn smiled at him. Exhaustion flooded back in, having been pushed aside by the thrill of flirting with a handsome man. Elbow to the table, she slumped over, head in her hand. "Sorry."

"Tired?" His lips thinned when she nodded. "You done eatin' then?"

"Yeah." She laughed softly. "Chewing is so much work, you know?"

He looked at her for a moment, then apparently came to a conclusion, because he nodded firmly and shoved his chair back. "Okay, up you get. Come on." Blade bent and gripped her hand, pulling Jenn to her feet and leading her away from the table. She followed him to her bedroom and watched in bemusement as he folded down her covers, each movement automatic and precise, as if he did this for her every day. "Come here," he called without looking up, making a final adjustment to the folded sheet.

"I'm here." She touched his shoulder. "You don't have to do this, Blade."

"If I did, I wouldn't. I'm contrary like that." He tipped his head sideways and smiled at her. "Lie down for a bit. We've got you cooled down, hydrated, and fed. Time to let Mother Nature do her recovery work."

The bed looked so welcoming she didn't argue, crawling up and tucking her feet under the sheet as she curled against the pillow. Blade drew the covers up to her shoulders, leaning over her.

Jenn smiled up at him. "Thank you."

With a hand on either side of her, he paused, seeming conflicted over something. She could see the moment when he mentally said *fuck it* and bent closer, his lips brushing her temple.

"Sleep well." He hadn't shifted backwards, and the movement of his lips brushing her skin was sensual and sweet. "I'll be here." Another soft kiss as her eyes drifted closed. The bed moved, and she snuggled deeper into the pillow. "So fuckin' pretty."

His words flashed through her head, the last thing she remembered before falling asleep with a smile on her lips.

Woman like you.

Nine

Blade

Shoulder to the doorframe, he watched her sleep. Deep and sweet, which was exactly what he'd hoped for. She'd needed it. Heat exhaustion was a bitch to get over, and she was fortunate to not have gotten a bad sunburn on top of everything else.

His phone buzzed with an incoming text. He was dressed, jeans and shirt, but barefooted. All their clothes were dry and hers were folded, and if he'd taken a couple extra minutes on her dainty underthings, he'd be the only one to know.

Digging the device out, he glanced at the screen and grinned before tapping out a quick response: **Tks. Owe you 1**.

Wolf had checked out her car, decided it'd be easier to fix at his shop, and had hauled it there with his wrecker. Her starter had gone bad, and Wolf could have it fixed by tomorrow. He said he'd found a spare key in a keeper attached to the inside of one wheel well, which made things easier. Blade would pick it up in the morning and bring it back. He was reluctant to give his brother her address, even if Wolf had probably already found it from her paperwork. This—being with her right here and now—was Blade's, and he wanted to keep it for himself.

Blade glanced at the windows, seeing the room reflected, the outside dark with no moon.

Jenn had been sleeping for more than five hours. The covers he'd tucked around her were exactly where he'd left them; she'd hardly moved in her sleep. He'd hustled around at first, wanting to get things tidied up before she woke. Before long, he'd had the food put away, dishes washed and dried, clothes moved from washer to dryer and then folded. Since then, he'd been here, less than ten feet away from the prettiest woman who'd ever spoken to him. Like some creeper, watching her sleep.

Pressing his lips together, he suppressed a sigh. *I'm such a fuckin' sap.*

He didn't move, though. Not physically. His mind was doing gymnastics, running through the day's events.

His unreasonable fear when he'd realized she was walking alone.

The feel of her on the bike behind him. Something he'd often wondered about but never experienced before today.

Her welcome weight against his chest as he held her in the bathtub.

That smile and giggle she'd given him at the dinner table.

Fuck, the way he felt just doing this—watching her sleep, without planning anything else. Not that he'd turn it down if she offered, but right now, just watching her, being here with her, filled him with a peace he hadn't known was missing. Each day filled with the struggle of recovery from the wreck, he'd been shocked to find there'd been a hole in his life he hadn't recognized, an empty space inside him that had gone unfilled—until Jenn. He ran a hand through his hair, fingers lingering and tracing along the thick scar behind his ear. She deserved a lot, so much more than him.

Since the accident, he saw himself as damaged, faulty in uncomfortable ways. The scar, the memory issues, his inability to work figures in his head or keep track of time, how his mouth failed him at the worst times, tension and stress stealing his voice. Flawed.

She deserved more.

But God, how he wanted.

"Hey."

Her voice pulled him from his thoughts, and he stared at her, hair tousled, eyes half-lidded and sleepy, smiling at him.

"Hey, yourself."

"What time is it?" She propped up on an elbow and twisted to look at the clock. The movement disturbed the covers, and they slipped to her waist, long lines of her body on display in the thin shirt she wore. "It's early yet. What are you doing up?" Throwing herself back onto the pillows, she groaned. "I hurt all over."

"You should book a massage." He thought about her car. "Do you work today?" She shook her head, stretching her arms overhead, the rustle of sheets against her skin a symphony of sensuality. Blood rushed to his cock when he imagined her moving like that underneath him, languid as he loved on her. "Uh. So...I'll have your car here by midday."

That earned him a cock of her head as she looked a silent question at him, one brow raised.

"I had a brother check it out." He tsked at her. "Spare key in the wheel well. Classic. It's a good thing you live in a low-crime county."

"My daddy had a saying. If they can live with it, I can live without it." She shrugged, her breasts rolling with the movement, and he lost track of what she was saying.

God, want my mouth on her. Want her under me in the worst way. Fuck, she's what I need. Everything I need, right there. Goddamned angel sent my way.

"...been a serious lack of issues, which is good." She pushed up on an elbow again, this time angled towards him, now frowning. "Blade, are you okay?"

He stared at her, mouth fused because the words were locked in his head again, just when he didn't want them to be, when he wanted more than anything to let them spill out, tell her what he was thinking.

"Blade?" She rose to her knees, the shirt slow to slip down her body, making his mouth water with the need to follow that same path. "You're scaring me." She stretched out a hand towards him, and he took a wobbling step, all balance gone.

Finally, his mouth decided to start working again, the sounds coming slowly, a torture of its own when he wanted to babble his thoughts to her. "You're just so goddamned everything, Jenn. I don't wanna screw anything up."

"Why do you assume you're going to screw up?" She took in a deep breath. "Ask me what I want, Blade. Go ahead, ask me."

He stood balanced on the knife's edge of uncertainty, afraid to ask a question where he didn't already know the answer, not when it mattered this much. *She wouldn't have said it like that if she was gonna blow me off*. He looked at her, smiling back at him, hand still outstretched. *Out of my league*. Her head tipped to the other side. *I don't care if she is. She's gonna be mine.*

"What do you want, Jenn?"

"You." Her answer was instant, no hesitation, voice low and throaty with desire. He took those final strides to the side of her bed and wrapped his fingers around hers, letting her pull him down.

Her skin was like silk under his hand as he caressed her cheek, thumb grazing across her lips. With her chin lifted in a clear invitation, he didn't make her wait long, swooping in to press a kiss to her mouth. Her pleased hum buzzed through him, and he returned for another one, and another, sweet closed-mouth caresses that had his whole body vibrating. Then her tongue touched his lips, a glancing quest of a touch, and it was on.

He spread her lips with his tongue, plunging in and sweeping, tangling with hers as he tasted her, drinking deep from her lips. She lay back on the pillows and he followed her down, pressed tight to her side, angling over her upper body to capture her mouth again, and again. The first touch of her hand on his arm made him groan into her mouth. Her fingers worked under the hem of the shirt, and he backed off a moment, reaching behind him to grip the neckband and strip if off over his head. Then it was back to Jenn, bodies pressed together, her hands exploring his back, shoulder, sides. He threaded his fingers through her hair, gripping and angling her mouth where he wanted it, and she moaned, arching up against him.

"You've got too many clothes on, Blade." He'd moved to her neck, kissing and nipping along that ivory column, and she pressed her lips next to his ear, the whisper and gust of breath making him shiver. "And, so do I."

"You're right." He sank his teeth into the notch of her shoulder and neck, gripping and holding for a moment, noting how her breathing changed to a quick pant, her voice thready when she responded.

"So, let's take care of that little problem."

"I'm enjoyin' myself right here." He ran his mouth along her collarbone, nosing underneath her shirt to get at more flesh, more skin, more heat. "But I see the advantages of your suggestion." Lifting up, he stared down at her. Cheeks flushed, lips parted, and the arousal he saw in her eyes had him bending for another slow, deep kiss. Wet and hot, their tongues tangled in a slide that made him want so much more. Murmuring against her mouth, he acquiesced, "Okay, strip."

From his position on his back next to her, he watched her undress, mostly under the blankets, as he shoved his jeans and briefs down his legs, kicking them off the bed. She finished and lay still, covers pulled up to the tops of her breasts, her eyes downcast slightly as if she were shy with him. He shuffled around and slipped into bed with her, then rolled so he was tight to her side, leaning over and studying her for a moment.

"This okay, Jenn?" He bent and nuzzled against her cheek, trying to ignore the demands of his rigid cock as he promised, "If you want to stop, just say the word. You're in control here. I'm all yours and all in on this, but if you wanna back off, there are no worries. Just say the word."

He'd made his way along her throat again, trailing kisses along the way, mixing them with a series of soft bites. Her skin was already reddened from his scruff, and he made a mental note to be more careful. Back at that sensitive juncture, he repeated the firm hold, sighing against her skin when she reacted the same way. This time the arch up brought with it the glorious glide of skin on skin, her breasts pressing against his chest.

"I want this, Blade."

With that go sign, he ventured farther, hand sliding up her side to cup a breast, lifting and plumping as he found the other with his mouth, pulling her deep on a hard draw, tongue flicking against the stiff bud of her nipple, her body shuddering and moving with each firm suck. Jenn's fingers carded through his hair, then gripped as she held him tightly against her. He fought and won the right to move to her other breast, treating it to the same loving attention until both nipples were pebbled and hard.

The covers tangled against his feet as he shifted between her thighs, and he kicked them down, the chill of the air conditioning a delicious contrast to the furnace her body created beneath him. He straightened his arms and lifted up, staring down at the perfection of Jenn. Full breasts reddened with nipples drawn into peaks, her belly rising and falling with her quick breaths, generous hips topping her shapely legs spread for him. Gaze back on her face, he saw she looked uncertain, bottom lip caught between her teeth.

"Fuckin' perfect, baby. Everything about you fits all of me." He rocked his hips, drawing his throbbing cock along her pussy, her lips separating and allowing him to slide in the slick wetness there. "Wanna eat you out before I get too carried away. Got me hard enough to pound nails, and I'm not sure I'll last. Wanna make this good for you."

"You don't have to." The sparkle in her eye put the lie to those words, and he smiled down at her, arching his back to drag his cock through her wet again.

He shifted down, tracing a path along her belly, dropping a chain of kisses from hip to hip before he lapped at her. When the first taste burst across his tongue, he groaned as it filled his mouth. Voice muffled against her flesh, he told her, "But I wanna. This isn't a chore, Jenn. This is part of me lovin' on you." He pressed a kiss to her clit, lips parting to suck on it lightly until her hips rose against him as she cried out. "Let me love on you, sweetheart."

"Sweetheart," she echoed, her voice wistful. "That's the first sweet name you've called me."

"Not in my head," he assured her, laving her with the flat of his tongue. "I didn't wanna offer myself the promise of this, not expecting you to want me the same way." Swirling circles over her clit with the tip of his tongue, he focused on that nub until her hips caught a demanding rhythm of movement. "Didn't wanna build myself up like that."

"Why would you—" Her breath caught and she moaned softly. "Why would you think I didn't want you?"

"You're you." He thought that covered all the reasons, but was wrong apparently, because she stiffened slightly and shifted. He looked up to see she'd lifted on her elbows and was frowning down at him. "What?"

"What does that mean? Is this more of that 'woman like you' bullshit you tried to give me earlier?" She stretched out a hand and trailed her fingers along the side of his face. "Why do you think that?"

"Out of my league." He put the words out there, wishing he could call them back an instant later. "But if you wanna slum it with me, I'll take every moment I can."

She pulled away and sat up, then reached for his head with both hands, drawing him close, pressing their foreheads together.

There was an intensity to her voice when she spoke, a vibrato that captured his attention and held it. "Would it surprise you to know I think the same, but of you? Look at you, Nate." He preened a little to hear her take ownership of his name like that. Then he focused on the rest of what she was saying. "You're smart, successful, have dozens of close friends who like and trust you, and you're gorgeous. Handsome beyond anything I'd ever expect to have in my bed. Your body is to die for, all those muscles and the strength. Your confidence." She drew him in for a kiss. "Trust me when I say this isn't slumming it. This is me reaching for the stars and hoping."

"I'm rough around the edges."

"You're sweet and loving."

"I'm not much of a cook."

"I can testify you make a mean sandwich."

"I'm not good with words anymore. My mouth doesn't work half the time."

"We seem to be communicating just fine."

Every argument he offered, she refuted, and each word wedged deeper into the crack she'd put in his defenses, breaking them down even more.

"You're so pretty."

"You're so handsome."

"You got an answer for everything, Jenn?"

"If it'll keep you in my bed, yes."

"You want this? Still? Want this with me?" His erection had flagged as they talked, but the touch of her fingers on his cock had him raging hard again in moments. He caught his breath as she curled her hand around the shaft, gripping him firmly as she jacked him slowly. "Guess that's a yes, then."

She laughed, the musical sound reverberating through him as it had every time, and he loved it.

"Yes, it's a yes, Nate."

"I like when you do that." He kissed her deep and slow, tongue stroking into her mouth following the rhythm she set—long, firm glides.

"Do what?"

The murmur against his lips was a distraction, so he caught her lip in his teeth, pulling off slowly. "Call me by my name. Here in bed, I think I wanna be Nate to you."

"Nate." Breaths ghosting across his mouth. "Nate." She dipped her head and pressed her lips to his neck, dragging a hot path down to his chest. "Nate." Chin up, she stared into his eyes as her fingers swiped across the head of his cock, then traveled to her mouth, the pink tip of her tongue curling around and lapping at the liquid she'd gathered. "Nate, make love to me."

She retreated, shifting to lie on her back, and he followed her down, stretching out at her side, mouth fused to hers as he captured each tiny gasp and moan. Fingers to the wet folds of her core, he plucked and stroked, caressing and thrumming until her hips moved restlessly, chasing each sensation. He paired two fingers and plunged inside, her hot pussy enveloping him as he set a fast pace, sliding in and out, thumb to her clit with a steady strum side to side.

Mouth open, she kept her gaze locked on his face, and he greedily catalogued every reaction, taking in her pleasure in what he was doing to her. Jenn's generous lips formed his name, "Nate." Then she was off, pushed over the precipice by his hands and lips, muscles of her body stringing tightly as she came hard.

Rolling to his side, he gathered her in his arms, holding her tight as she shook and shuddered, the aftershocks of her orgasm gradually drawing to a close as her breathing slowed.

"Condom's in my jeans." He kissed her temple. "I'll be right back." Her fingers clutched at his arm as she lifted her chin, then released as he kissed her softly. "Stay here."

"Like I'm going anywhere." Her eyes closed, and a smile curved her lips when he glanced over his shoulder. "That was good."

Crinkly wrapper in hand, he turned to face the bed, cock jutting out at right angles from his body. He stared at her and curled his fingers around his dick, pumping up and down a few times as he let his gaze travel along her form.

"Jenn." Neither a question nor a statement; he simply said her name and waited until she opened her eyes. "I like you."

Gaze flicking from where his hand worked his cock up to his eyes, her expression grew somber. "I like you, too." Lying partly on her side, she shoved a hand under her head and lifted, staring at him. "A lot."

"You still want me?"

Her legs spread slightly, and he saw glistening moisture on her pussy lips. Stomach clenching, he waited for her response, trembling with anticipation.

She didn't make him wait long.

Ten

Jenn

"Make love to me." Heart in her throat, she waited for Nate to react. The smile that lifted the corners of his lips was beautiful to see. Telling him how she felt had been scary, but getting it back from him had thrilled her.

This man, this gorgeous specimen of a man who stood before her, wasn't turned off by the idea of more. From the way his erection strained towards her, he was the opposite of turned off.

She watched as he stroked his cock again, then made quick work of putting on the condom before stalking back to the bed. He shifted in beside her and then, with a fluid movement, covered her as Jenn reached for him, pulling

Nate down and into her arms. Cheek to cheek, she listened to the hitch in his breath as he rolled his hips, the head of his cock slipping into place so naturally it was as if they'd done this a hundred times. The shivery thrill inside her at being with him like this, holding him, feeling the strength of his body as he surrounded her—she hoped that would never fade.

He thrust as she raised her hips, and his cock glided home inch by inch, a steady push that filled and stretched her until he was as deep as he could go, hips grinding into hers.

Nate shoved his face against her neck, breathing gone harsh and heavy as he groaned out her name. His hips moved in little pulses, pulling back and plunging inside, repeating until they were both covered in sweat. Hands playing along his back and sides, she caressed every inch of him she could reach, keeping rhythm with his movements, lifting and arching against him.

He murmured her name like a mantra, soft and reverent. Interspersed were broken phrases, sentence fragments strung together on shallow breaths, and she loved knowing she was doing this to him.

"Jenn. God, Jenn." His hand slipped up her side, fingers and thumb meeting at her nipple as he tugged and rolled. "So fuckin' good. Good to me. You, with me like this. God. Deep in you. Tight and, tight, so fuckin' tight. Giving. To me, give this." His chin nudged at hers, and she arched her neck, granting him better access. "Mark you." Teeth grazed along her neck, flesh soothed by a trailing pass from his tongue. "Mine. Want you to be mine." Each phrase was punctuated by a hard thrust, driving deep, shaking her to her core. "Only me. Just me." His lips found hers with a wet, fierce kiss, Nate possessing her fully. "Be mine. God. So good, what you do. Just me."

"You want me to be yours?" At her words, his hips slapped against hers and he ground into her, pelvic bone hard against her clit. Air burst from him as he shoved his arms under her back, clutching her to his chest, and he buried his face against her neck again. "Want that, Nate? I want that, too. So much. I want to belong." As she said the words, she realized they were a deep truth she'd never looked at too closely. "Want to be yours and no one else's. Want to love you, and be loved." She wrapped her arms around his neck, turning her head to whisper into his ear, "When I said I liked you, I wasn't lying. I like you a lot, Nate. I want to be yours."

He groaned deep and low, the edges of the sound jagged with lust. The whole time she held tight as his hips snapped forwards, driving his cock deep. Pounding hard until he stayed planted, another groan breaking free from his chest, and his body jolted. "You're fuckin' mine." His arms squeezed, biceps flexing as he tightened his hold on her and filled the condom, his cock pulsing hotly inside her.

Jenn curved her limbs around every piece of Nate she could reach, pulling until the space between them was gone. Joined as they were, she could feel every shift of his body, every breath he took. Cheek pressed to his bristly one, she held her breath, letting the stroking passes of his hands on her skin build her courage. Finally, she released a gasp, felt the rumble of his questioning hum. "If I'm yours..." The words hung in the air until she finished, taking ownership of him and this fragile thing they were building together. "Then you're mine."

Eleven

Blade

"No, man." He shook his head as he lifted the cold beer to his lips. Speaking against the lip of the bottle, he admitted his greatest fear. "There's no reason for her to pick me. My gut tells me to hold back because it's only a matter of time." Today was a good talking day, the words flowing as easily as the beer did. He leaned an elbow against the table and looked up at Monk. "I ask myself why would she settle when she could have the world?"

"Why do you see it as settling?" Monk tipped his head to the side, a puzzled expression on his face. "You tell her about the wreck yet? That's something you need to share, and you know it. Won't matter to her. From what you've said, she already knows you're a catch."

He shrugged. "Not yet. It's not my favorite topic. You of all people should understand. You picked my ass up off the floor enough, man. She's fuckin' perfect, and I'm...me." Draining the bottle, he glanced at Monk's to see the level had hardly moved. "Drink up, brother. I'll get us a couple more."

"Nah, man. I'm good. Gonna head out with some prospects soon. Ride up front, flash the patch. Gotta give 'em something to chase, ya know?" Monk settled in his chair, arm slung over the back. "Let's get back to the part where you somehow think you're less than desirable and that if the woman decided to be with you, she'd be selling herself short."

"I don't think." He pushed his chair backwards and stood. "I know."

"Don't assume we won't continue this conversation, asshole," Monk called after him, and Blade lifted his hand over his shoulder, flipping him off.

When he was back in his chair with a beer, Monk sat in silence for a minute, waiting until Blade had a mouthful before he began again. "Out of anybody she could have picked, she's set her sights on you."

Blade grunted and nodded, swallowing hard. "Yeah, I don't get it either."

"You mistake me, motherfucker." Monk leaned in, tapping the table with a stiffened finger. "Who the fuck are you to say what she gets to feel? Huh? That's not your place, man. She likes you, or doesn't…that's hers, not yours. And if she *wants* to pick you? Regardless of how you don't feel worthy or some shit, if you wanna pick her back, then you fuckin' go for it, brother. You go for it and you hold tight to that shit." He reached out and thumped the backs of his knuckles against Blade's chest. "You nearly fuckin' died. She could die tomorrow."

Acid burned up the back of Blade's throat, and he opened his mouth to shout down Monk's words. Monk cut him off with a brusque headshake.

"Brother, you know it could happen. Amanda's husband didn't make it back. He died overseas and left her alone. You had a stupid fuckin' bitch mow you down with her car, and if the worst had happened, might never have met your Jenn." Amanda was a war widow Monk had taken an interest in a while ago. They'd gone from only meeting at her dead husband's grave to texting, and Blade believed it was only a matter of time before Monk pulled his head out of his ass and took it a step farther. "If you have a chance at a single moment with her and it's something you both want, then why the fuck would you deny her that, brother? You take hold and make sure if it's only a single fuckin' moment, that it's the best goddamned moment in her life. You take hold, for her. For you." Another hard thump against his chest. "For you, brother. Because you do deserve her. She wants you? Don't let her go, then. You take hold."

He sat back with a huff, angling his chin to the side.

"Look at you, givin' me grown-up advice like that." Blade cleared his throat. "Turn a little of that on yourself, brother. You and Amanda, it's a done deal, my man. You tell me to take hold?" Monk nodded, his eyes still aimed somewhere over Blade's shoulder. "I'm telling you to let go that hold you have on yourself and trust that she'll catch you when you fall. Let go and trust. I'll hold if you do that. Can you do that for me, brother?"

"We're a couple of fuckin' saps, man." Monk's eyes cut sideways as he grinned.

Blade returned the smile, adding a nod. "Sugar sweet, that's us."

***

Jenn

She curled her legs up beside her on the couch, leaning back and studying Blade's face. "You're kinda scaring me," she admitted, struggling to keep her voice even. He'd called a half an hour ago and asked if they could talk. The words sounded so much like a lead-in to the dreaded brush-off that it was all her mind would let her focus on. Now that he was here, the tension in his expression was palpable.

"I didn't. I didn't mean to, Jenn." Brow furrowed, he shook his head. "I got something. I need to tell you." Sentences broken and staccato, he told her a little more about the seriousness of whatever topic this was supposed to be with every word. "Shoulda already."

"I'm here." She slid her hand towards him, palm down on the cushions. "I'm listening."

He reached out almost desperately, covering her hand with his own and clutching tightly at her fingers.

"I'm not one to talk. Not much about my feelings." His gaze searched her face, settling on her lips, and she gave him a shaky smile he returned. "But between Monk and my therapist, they convinced. They convinced me to talk to you."

A therapist? She managed to keep the words in her head, only barely, giving him a shallow nod of encouragement.

"I was in a wreck. I wrecked out. On the bike." Blade closed his eyes, and a muscle in his jaw clenched. "A drunk hit me and nearly. She nearly killed me."

"Oh my God." Jenn's reaction was soft, the words breathed in shock. "When?"

"Not long ago. A while, but I'm still recovering." That muscle in his jaw muscle flexed and shook. "I have problems with my head. My head and my mouth. Math. Reading. Speaking." His fingers squeezed hers in a slow rhythm. Tighten, relax. "My words don't work all the time."

Jenn flashed back to a few statements he'd made through their time together, slowly beginning to piece together the self-deprecating cut-downs he'd applied to himself. Shifting closer to him, she reached up with the hand he hadn't claimed and trailed her fingertips along his cheek. She threaded them through his hair, navigating by feel until she came to the ridged scar behind his ear that he'd avoided talking about. *Until now.* "This." She leaned closer, holding still until he opened his eyes. She saw the flare of his pupils, then the heat she'd come to expect whenever they were together. "This is from that accident, isn't it? This scar?"

"Brain surgery number two." His lips pursed on the final word, and she darted forwards to place a kiss against them, liking how he showed her his surprise with a quick indrawn breath. "I was so busted up, Jenn. You wouldn't have. Wouldn't have recognized me. Hell, Monk has photos from the first days. I don't recognize myself. Tubes everywhere. Face so swollen my eyes wouldn't open even if I'd been awake."

"You were in a coma?" Even with the effort she put into steadying her voice, the final word broke a little, and he winced. "Blade. Nate. You're okay now, right?"

"Some things are good." He shrugged and moved closer, his thigh against her legs when he turned to face her. "Some things are as good as they're gonna get. My mouth." His lips clamped shut and his mouth twisted to the side. "My mouth comes and goes. The words. The nightmares. Those are better when I'm with you. But what you see is what you get."

"Well..." She straightened her spine, staring at him. "You had brain surgery. More than one. I think the fact you're walking and talking at all is a miracle." She traced along the scar again, glad he was letting her touch him like this. "The fact I get to have you, to hold you—that's another miracle, Nate."

"I'm always going to struggle. There's a lot that can't be fixed."

"I don't think you need to be fixed, Nathanael. I like you just the way you are." Jenn angled her head to touch his, foreheads pressed together. "My miracle man."

"Jesus, Jenn. Do you even know how special you are?"

"Do I get to keep you? Are you mine?" He nodded, but she noted he was careful not to break that contact between them. "If you're mine, then that's all that matters."

Twelve

Jenn

Purse in hand, Jenn tossed a wave over her shoulder to Rose as she made her way out through the door. She normally worked days, but one of the other waitresses had called in sick, so the manager had asked Jenn to fill in. As the door closed behind her, Jenn shivered. It was one of the few nights a week the diner was open until midnight, capturing traffic from a couple of bars near the county line. The parking lot was dark, and the shadows cast by the shed and cars turned everything unfamiliar and somehow menacing.

She glanced down as she dug for her keys, startled when a voice called out from the shadows next to the shed. She looked up, searching the darkness. "Hello?" She didn't see anyone, no movement, and the sound didn't repeat, so she hurried to her car, clicking the fob as she reached the door.

Sliding behind the wheel, she breathed a heavy sigh of relief. *That was creepy.* The car started easily, and she pulled out of the parking lot, heading home and sending a silent thanks to Blade's friend Wolf. He'd worked on her car three times now, each at his insistence, pointing out things that were likely to become problems and cutting her a deep discount to have the repairs done.

In town, she made a stop at the local grocery store. Factories in town meant they kept hours convenient to shift workers, which was a boon on a night like tonight. A quick turn through the fruits and vegetables with basket in hand, then the dairy section for more cream, and a stop at an endcap touting a special, and she was back at the front checking out.

Back in the store's parking lot, she looked around, confused. She'd exited the store and angled directly to where she always parked—and certainly had just done so— but her car was nowhere to be seen. Jenn stumbled to a stop as she fumbled with her purse and bags, retrieving her keys. A click of the fob had her head jerking to the side as a car's horn beeped in response. On the opposite side of the lot, her car was backed into a lined slot against a neighboring business.

Jenn approached the car cautiously; she knew she hadn't parked here. It required backing, and that was a maneuver she tried to avoid. She crowded close to the wall as she sidled towards the car, angling her head to look into the shadowy back seat to find it empty, as was the front.

"Very funny." She looked around, expecting to see someone jump out with an announcement that she'd been punked, but there was no one. Glancing over her shoulder, she opened the back door and placed her groceries on the floor. They were flimsy, reusable bags, and one of them tipped over, spilling the contents, glass jars of pasta sauce clinking against the jug of creamer. "Dammit."

When she stood up from straightening the mess and looked around again, she yelped aloud because there was a motorcycle parked in front of her car, wheel pointed towards her bumper. Panicked, she took a moment to recognize the rider, and air whooshed out of her when she saw it was Blade. "Oh, God. You scared me."

He dismounted, leaning the bike on the kickstand before walking to her. The smile on his face wasn't gleeful, not as if he'd played a prank on her by moving the car. The expression on his face was soft and sweet, one that said seeing her was a welcome surprise. "Hey." He crowded close and dipped his head to brush his lips against hers. "I didn't expect to find you here."

Heart still pounding, she lifted to her toes to chase his mouth, rewarded with a deep chuckle and a deeper kiss. "I'm headed home." She leaned against his chest when he wrapped his arms around her, letting his strength support her. "Wanna come for a visit?"

The heat in his eyes was instant, and a surge of need rippled through her belly, zinging between her legs. His breathing changed, deepening, and she saw his focus shift to her mouth. "Yeah," he said, voice low and guttural. "I want."

He followed her home, pulled the bike up next to the house, and met her at the car door to load up his hands with the grocery bags. Jenn protested, unsuccessfully, and quickly resigned herself to opening doors instead of carrying food.

Putting away the groceries was a different kind of exercise with Blade helping. Different didn't mean bad. Not at all. He quickly commandeered retrieval of each item, and when he would pass it to her, he would hold tight until she paid his self-proclaimed kiss tariff. Each kiss was sweeter than the last, hotter, wet and deep, until she found herself crowded against the countertop, Blade plastered to her front, his hands buried in her hair. She angled her chin up, opening herself for exploration from his mouth. Her breath caught in her throat as he mouthed her neck, his teeth, lips, and the burn of his scruff ratcheting up her desire to fever pitch.

"Let's move this to the bedroom." His arms were tight around her, holding her in place, and she didn't try to escape. Something about Blade's ability to make her want him fractured her control, short-circuiting any semblance of self-preservation, until all she could think of was him owning her body, him inside, him with her.

"Yes." Jenn was shocked at the sound of her own voice, rough and needy, but Blade didn't seem to mind if the pleased rumble in his chest was any indication.

"Kiss me," he demanded as he scooped her up, arms banded around her upper thighs and back, holding her to his chest. She wrapped her arms around his neck, offering her mouth, and he swooped down the tiny distance separating them, tongue sweeping in and tangling with hers.

He laid her gently on the bed, then pounced, making her giggle as she bounced when he landed on all fours over her. Moving slowly, he stretched out over her, blanketing her with heat and pressure, his weight enough to make her ribs strain to pull in a full breath. Then he kissed her again, and she was short of breath for another reason, his hand on her breast a caress pulling strings connecting to her core, making her hips jerk up. His rigid cock, trapped behind the zipper of his jeans, still branded her like an ember. Fingers tightened in her hair as Blade moved his mouth to her throat, her shoulder, her breast over the clothing she still wore. He held her in place, and Jenn felt ravished in all the best ways, his open desire for her an aphrodisiac she hadn't expected.

"Jenn." He groaned her name, mouth pressed to the skin above her shirt, lips and teeth making her quiver under him. "Clothes off, yeah?"

"Yeah." When he rose up on stiffened arms, she went for the fastening on his jeans, careful with the zipper as she shoved them halfway down his thighs, until his cock bounced free.

"Jenn." This was a roughened whisper, and she dragged her gaze from where she'd wrapped her hand around his cock and up to his face. Eyes closed, he had his bottom lip caught in a savage grip between his teeth, face twisted in a ferocious snarl. "Goddammit, woman."

Wondering how far he'd let her go, she looked back to where she held him as she stroked down, then back up, tightening her grip around the sensitive crown, feeling the pebbled ridge as it passed over her fingers. She swiped across the head, not surprised to find slippery fluid leaking from his slit. His hips jerked and plunged, cock fucking through her hand, and she stroked down and up again.

Blade shifted suddenly, hips retreating until her hand was empty, and she glanced up to see the snarl had been replaced by an expression of such intensity it froze the air in her lungs. Blade was focused on her, unblinking, looking nearly feral.

"Gonna. Gotta be in you." He stripped her quickly, then shucked the rest of his clothes, until they were both naked. He moved over her again, that heated blanket she could learn to love. "You on the pill?"

Jenn nodded. "Yeah. Injections, but yeah, I'm covered with birth control."

He groaned and dropped his mouth to her chest, his lips unerringly finding and latching onto a nipple, alternating sucking hard with the torment of tiny bites. "I'm tested."

She knew what he wanted. Something she'd never done with a partner before. *I've never felt like this before.* With that reasoning in mind, Jenn very deliberately spread her legs in an invitation he couldn't mistake. Blade didn't disappoint. He fell into the cradle created for him with a lithe twist of his hips. Another shift of position had his cock poised at her entrance, and Jenn held her breath, waiting.

Lips pressed to hers, he thrust his tongue into her mouth at the same time he slid inside. His back arched under her palms, and she rolled her hips up to take him deep. Whispering his name when he was seated inside as far as he could go, she held still, muscles quivering as she grazed a gentle touch up his arms, curling around his shoulders and up his neck, tangling in his hair. "Nate. Baby, move."

"Oh, God." His groan echoed through the air, and he *moved*.

They came together in a crash of flesh, sweat coating their skin to create a slippery canvas painted by their fingertips. She gasped to the symphony of the sounds of his cock plunging deep and pulling back, thrusting inside hard and fast. When she came, it surprised her, the buildup fast and hard, bowing her back as she scrabbled for a hold on his skin, his flesh, his body—his being. He seemed to understand what she was waiting for, and mouth to her ear, he set her free to fly. "Go, baby. Take what you need. Come all over me. I got you. I'll always, always have you. Go. Take it."

Her vision darkened on the edges, breathing suspended for long moments until her lungs protested, sucking in another draught of air before seizing again.

Nate—because he wasn't Blade in this moment, as he'd asked her, as she'd done instinctively, she'd transformed him to Nate as soon as he'd started loving on her— groaned, the sound harsh, cut off as he buried his face against her throat, setting his teeth in the muscle in the notch of her shoulder. His hips bucked, drawing his cock out until she nearly lost him. The swollen rim pushed back inside a dozen times, spreading her, stretching her in pulsing pumps. Then he was deep inside again, so deep he ground against her clit, his sac brushing the cheeks of her ass, and he came. Heat filled her, a delicious feeling of something forbidden as she'd never allowed this, never experienced the extra slipperiness, the sense of overfilling as his cock throbbed and throbbed.

Her orgasm was passing, slipping away like an elusive scent on the wind, and she clenched down hard as she tried to extend it, surprised by Nate's reaction. He pushed both hands underneath her, cupping her ass and lifting while he pounded hard for another handful of thrusts, her name a groaned sound against her skin.

"So fuckin' good." His fingers tightened their grip, and she arched, lifting for him. "God, Jenn."

"Was pretty good from my side, too." She fought to catch her breath, each word coming out on an individual huff of air. "Really good."

"Glad you clarified." He chuckled, and she felt the rumbling shake down to her bones, his position on top of her pressing the humor into her skin. "Otherwise I might develop a complex about being only pretty good."

"Liar. You know you're more than really good, even." Turning her head, she kissed his cheek softly. "Overwhelmingly good."

That pleased chuckle rolled through her again, and she saw the curve of his cheek when he smiled. "I guess I don't have to ask if it was good for you?" He lifted slightly and pulled out, moving to his back on the bed next to her. A moment later, he hooked his arm around her neck and yanked her towards him, positioning her half on top of his chest.

She angled her arm, chin resting in her hand. "So good."

"I've never had it that good, Jenn. Never had anything close. Wanna know what I spent the day thinking?" Lips pressed together, she nodded. "How I could prove. Prove to you that I. That I was good enough. That I'd be worth. Worth takin' a chance on." He looked frustrated, brow furrowing. "My mouth." Huffing out a sigh, he shook his head. "This is. It is how it is. Some. Days are better. Better than others."

Jenn lifted a hand and cupped his cheek. "I don't care."

"You will." The bleak expression that fleeted across his features broke her heart, and she shook her head fiercely.

"You don't get to tell me what I want. You can't decide that for me. If you don't like me, or don't want me around, then that's your decision. But if you want this? Want this with me? Then you can't try to predetermine the ending. Nate, baby, we've hardly begun. I can't wait to see where this takes us, because it feels so very right to me, but don't put some kind of time limit on this just because you're afraid." He jerked at that word and she nodded. "Oh, I know. You're this military guy, been in a dozen firefights, because your friends do like to brag on you, mostly because you won't brag on yourself. But in this, you're letting some false sense of unworthiness make you afraid. Don't be afraid of winning."

"I get so." His face twisted into an unpleasant expression, an unwelcome echo of his previous one. He lifted a hand and thumped it solidly against the side of his head once, then a second time. He'd pulled back for a third strike when she curled her fingers around his wrist, staying the blow. "So frustrated."

"If I tell you I'm not, would you believe me?" Gazes locked, they stared at each other for a long minute. Then he slowly shook his head side to side. "Then I'll have to prove it to you." Digging her toes into the mattress, she pushed up until she could kiss him, pressing her lips against his. With a sigh, she relaxed back against his chest, laying her cheek on his pec and gazing into his face. "I'm listening, Nate. I'll be here."

His arms tightened around her, squeezing down like bands of steel, holding her in place. Voice rough and hesitant, he whispered something that wasn't as much a secret as he seemed to believe. "I think I love you."

Jenn smiled at him through the sheen of tears his unexpected bomb had caused, fingers drawing tiny circles on his chest, not moving a muscle otherwise. "I know I love you."

He huffed out a laugh, then sighed deeply, tension flowing out of his muscles with the breath.

"Can you believe me, Nate? Believe this is real now?"

"I'll try."

"That's the right answer."

Thirteen

Blade

Shirtless, he was scooping coffee into the machine's filter the next morning, not yet awake, when Jenn's arms slipped around his waist.

Last night had moved up every space on the list to become the best in his life, setting the bar so high he didn't know if there'd ever be a contender to upset its reign. Honestly, he didn't care. Jenn filled every hole he didn't know he'd had inside, fitting into place beside him seamlessly. Even with the distance of a couple hours' sleep, it didn't matter. This was the woman for him. The only one he'd ever love, and he was honored she'd offered the emotion right back to him. More proof that they were better together than apart.

No time like the present. The conversation he wanted to have would show her exactly where he was in this. Would prove his trust in what they were building together. "What if I asked you to make room in your closet for me?"

"New York minute." She gave him a squeeze, cheek resting between his shoulder blades. "Half the drawers in the dresser, too? You got it."

"Can it be that easy?" He finished with the coffee maker and thumbed the switch to start the process. Turning in her arms, he wrapped his around her shoulders, pulling her close. He dipped down for a kiss that she met halfway. Rolling up to her toes caused her whole body to slide against his, and the softness of her breasts and belly were brands of heat against his skin.

"Easy as we make it." She shrugged and settled on her heels, that glorious slide happening again in reverse. "Hey, I forgot to tell you that was mean yesterday."

"What?" He wracked his brain to sort out what she was talking about, coming up with nothing. "What'd I do?" Chasing her mouth for another kiss, he nipped her bottom lip gently. "How was I mean?"

"That whole move-the-car thing." She shifted so her hands were resting on his chest and thudded him softly with a fist. "It really scared me."

"What are you talking about?" The coffee maker gurgled and spit, the only sound in the room. "Jenn?"

"You didn't move my car at the grocery store?" Blade shook his head. "Are you sure? Maybe Wolf?"

"He was at the clubhouse when I left there. I was riding by the parking lot when I saw you walking to your car, Jenn. What do you mean, moved it?" His gut tensed, sending spikes of alarm throughout his body, the same kind of instinctive reaction he'd experienced so many times over in the sandbox, just before the world would turn upside down and bleed red. "I didn't do anything to the car."

"When I came out of the grocery store, I could swear my car wasn't where I left it. I'd never back it into a spot like that. And I shop there a lot, nearly always park on the other side of the lot." She pressed closer to him, and he realized she was trembling. "When you showed up like you did, I assumed you'd done it. You know where I keep the spare key."

"Did you notice anything? Anything unusual when you came outside? Or went in? Anything odd at all happen yesterday?" She shook her head, then paused, a considering expression on her face. "What? What are you thinkin' about?"

"There was this moment when I got off work. I thought I heard someone behind the diner." Jenn shrugged and laughed, the sound coming out strangled and pained. "You know how it is back there. The woods are close, and it can be really dark at night. I wasn't scared, not really. Just spooked as hell. I got in the car and left, then stopped at the store."

"You think someone might have been out back of the diner last night?" She stared at him a moment; then her mouth twisted to the side and she nodded slowly. "Who else worked until close last night?"

"Rose did."

"Call her." He issued the order immediately, not giving Jenn time to think. "Make sure she's okay. Don't freak her out. Just make up something." White filled her face, and he saw her chin quiver. With her gaze fixed on him, she didn't move until he gripped her waist and set her back a half a foot. "Go, call her."

"Okay."

He stared at Jenn's ass as she trotted up the hallway to her bedroom, losing sight of her as she rounded the doorframe. That sense of unease intensified by the moment, and he glanced at the door to see the chain unlatched, the lock unengaged. *Did I not lock up last night?* They'd come in and Jenn had opened the door. Then he'd made a game of putting up her groceries before carrying her into the bedroom like a caveman. *Maybe, maybe not.* He felt naked without a weapon, but his gun was in one of the bags on his bike, and he wanted to sweep the house fast. Deadbolt engaged, he turned to see Jenn walking back into the kitchen, phone to her ear.

"Hey, Rose." The relief in her voice was palpable. "Do you know if I work today? I forgot to check the schedule." A pause, then she laughed. "Then I'm taking a lazy day.

Thanks, honey. Everything okay last night?" Another pause, this one longer, but Jenn's expression never changed, not showing any alarm. "Oh, cool. I'm glad it was an easy night. I'll see you soon." She sighed. "Yeah, you too. Bye." She laid the phone on the counter with a shake of her head. "She said everything was normal. Blade, what are you thinking?"

"I don't know. What to think yet. But I need. You to stay. Right. Here." Adrenaline caused his mouth to misfire, making the sentence a series of running starts and stops. He gripped her shoulders and moved her into position next to the door. "If I tell you. Tell you to go outside. You do just that." Pushing her car keys into one hand, he wrapped her fingers around the phone with the other, gripping them tightly. "And you get in the car. And you go to Wolf's garage. He'll be there. Even this early."

"Blade, you're scaring me." Pupils wide, she stared at him, gaze darting back and forth between his eyes.

"I'm just going to check out. A couple of things." Brushing his lips across hers, he felt her trembling breath. "Make sure we're good. Good here." Straightening and looking down at her, he slipped the length of his belt from the loops around his waist. Curling the leather around his fist until he had a short length left, topped by the metal buckle, he gave her a wink and a smile he didn't feel. "Back in a minute."

Stalking room-by-room earned him nothing except a more thorough knowledge of her floor plan and furniture placement. *Nothing.* In the living room, he tested the front door and found it locked tightly. Shaking his head over how his gut had misled him, he lifted one corner of the curtain over the wide windows and saw a shape directly in front of the house. *Her car.* Something looked off, and he squinted through the misty shadows of predawn.

There was something written on the windows.

Door hanging open behind him, a moment later Blade stood next to her car, scowling down at the words scrawled in white across every glass surface of the car.

Bitch you gonna pay.

The initial thought in his head was the first night he'd met Jenn. That moment in back of the diner when he'd realized what the club's prospects were up to, and how he'd stopped it before it went any further than attempted intimidation.

But the two men had lost their vests, any chance of earning a patch removed along with the denim. Something they'd been working towards, gone in a moment. Gibby had told him a couple days later that he'd taken it further, making a call to every dominant support club within a reasonable distance, blacklisting the two men.

That's it. It had to be.

"Blade?" He turned to find Jenn standing on the small cement porch. "What's going on?"

"I don't know." He wasn't lying, because nothing was certain. Just his gut speculating on things with his brain, coming to their own conclusions. "I'm going to find out." He reached out and found the white letters were still wet. Lifting his finger to his nose, he sniffed, taking in the acrid scent of acrylic. *Paint.* "I'll call Wolf. He's got something that can help get this off. Hopefully without fuckin' with your finish." That would give him a chance to bring his brothers up to speed, because if this was the work of those ex-prospects, then Jenn would gain protection from the entire club, not just Blade. "Go back inside, Jenn. The house is safe."

Phone to his ear, he'd turned away from her and didn't hear her approach. Her hit against his back was a surprise, and Blade whirled, unconsciously reacting with an arm cocked back for a powerful blow. He dropped his fist and stared at her.

She wasn't daunted, not losing any of her anger at the unintentional threat he'd offered. "No. You don't do that, Blade. This is my car, and our house." Her easy acceptance of what he'd voiced earlier was a shock, and he stood there, mouth open. "And you won't just go off and figure it out on your own."

"Yo." Wolf's voice in his ear told him the call had gone through.

Jenn tossed her hair back, chin lifted stubbornly. "If you think you're going to act a Neanderthal all the time, you need to think again. In the bedroom is one thing, but out here we'll have conversations like real grown-ups."

He spoke over Wolf's laughter at her words. "Just a second, brother." Resting the phone against his chest, he stared down at Jenn. "I'm gonna fix this. It's what I do, Jenn. That's me, down to my soul. I'm...I'm a fixer and a man. A man who makes things right. You're gonna have to give me this one. I'm not going off on my own. I've already got Wolf on the phone. I promise you. We'll talk about it later. But right now, I need to fix this."

"You know who it was?" The uplift of her voice was a formality, because he saw the certainty in her gaze.

"I think so."

"It was those men, wasn't it? The ones who harassed me?" He nodded. "Assholes. No means no, and they need a lesson they won't forget." She tipped her head to one side and studied him, gaze traveling down and back up, landing on his face. Her voice was softer when she asked him, "Are you going to teach them that lesson, Blade?"

"Sure am, honey." He didn't question her about-face, not sure if the reversal was due to his statement of need or her recognition that if it *was* the ex-prospects, then he'd feel guilty by association if he didn't make it right. He didn't care, as long as Jenn let him do this and didn't hate him for it.

"Then talk to Wolf, and talk to Gibby, and tell me what you need from me." She glanced at the car and shook her head. "Not just assholes, but stupid. Did they not see your bike parked right there?" Jenn whirled and stomped back to the front door. She stepped over the threshold and paused, turning back to look at him. Her words belied her angry expression when she cooed, "I love you, Nate."

"I love you, too." She closed the door and he listened to the silence for a moment before lifting his voice to call out, "Lock the door, honey." He heard the click as the lock engaged, then the curtains on the window fluttered, her hand appearing with one uplifted finger. Well, maybe she wasn't entirely okay, but she was somewhat okay. *I'll take it.*

Lifting the phone again, he was surprised to still hear Wolf's laughter. Between wheezes of hard-won breath, he heard the man choking out. "I love you too, honey."

"Fuck you."

"Not my type."

"You're not mine, either." He pulled in a slow, steadying breath. "FNGs we cut a few weeks ago, I think they've targeted Jenn." Wolf fell silent and Blade kept talking, fighting to get through the unnatural pauses and stuttering words as he went back through everything he knew or suspected.

There was a long moment of silence when he finished, then Wolf whistled low. "I'll call Gibby and talk to him. If they know where she lives, you need to stay there, brother. Stay on her, keep her safe. I'll get Neptune and we'll come to you, bring a probie to drive the car back to the shop."

"Where's Monk?" It was telling that Wolf hadn't mentioned him.

"Off chasin' his ghost." That meant the widow he'd become obsessed with.

"Okay. Texting you the address." He tapped it out, pressed Send, and quickly heard the ding of a bell in the background as it came through on Wolf's end.

"Got it. See you soon, brother."

Blade disconnected the call, staring at the woods just beyond the driveway. There could be a dozen men hiding there, and he'd never know. He retrieved his gun from the bike, relieved to find it still there. Either they hadn't seen the bike—not too much of a stretch since he'd parked in the shadows intentionally—or they hadn't given a shit, something he didn't believe for one minute. Regardless, everything was still where he'd left it. He glanced back at the words scrawled on her car, the fury roaring back in an instant. *Won't save 'em. Don't give a shit.* They'd threatened Jenn, and she was his. "Cannot stand."

He turned and strode to the door, lifting his hand to knock. It opened before he could connect, and then he had an armful of soft and sweet-smelling woman, albeit an angry one.

Fourteen

Blade

With his arms folded across his chest, Blade looked down the five steps to the backyard of the clubhouse, where Wolf and Monk each gripped a shoulder of the men kneeling in front of them. In the flickering light of torches and firepit, he saw the two restrained men carried visibly bloodied and bruised marks from their time with his brothers, something that settled a tiny part of Blade's rage.

It was less than a day since the assholes had started their ill-conceived idea of terrorizing Jenn. Surveillance footage from the diner and grocery store's systems had given Gibby all the club needed to know to determine who the bad actors were. He'd pulled Blade in a couple of hours ago to tell him they were bringing the two men to the clubhouse and asked for his approval on how to handle the situation.

That consideration had been a nod to Jenn's place in Blade's life, no matter she didn't have a Protected by patch yet. She would, and Gibby knew it.

Terror dealt to Jenn would be met with terror, and their physical mistreatment of her would be matched by what they'd endure.

And Blade didn't give one single flying fuck what it said about him that he was looking forward to it.

"How you want to do this, brother?" Gibby's quiet question wasn't to benefit their trusted members arranged in a rough semicircle around the men. Blade let his lip curl in a sneer as he stared down at the two ex-prospects. From the widening of their eyes, whites showing, the prearranged tactic was working.

"Hard." The man on the left tried to jerk free of Wolf's hold, but with wrists bound behind him, he quickly found himself yanked back upright, made to look up at where Blade stood next to Gibby. "One of 'em put their hands on a woman. Hard enough to mark her throat. Marked her. On a club run." He shook his head. "That shit cannot stand."

"What woman?" Neptune's question was right on cue, and Blade angled his head towards his brother in thanks.

"Woman at the diner. Waitress just doin' her job." Teeth gritted, he forced out the next part of the script. "Woman says no. A man's got an obligation. Obligation to leave her the fuck alone."

"The woman, this waitress, did she say no?" Wolf's man tried again to pull free and was met with a more forceful response.

Blade waited until Wolf had the man on his knees again before he answered, letting the silence drag out for long moments as the man cleared dirt and grass from his mouth, spitting and hacking, bending his head to the side as blood flowed freely from a cut that had opened over one eye.

"You asked if she said no." He lifted his chin, unfolding his arms so his clenched fists hung at his sides. "She did." He took a step forwards, balancing his boots on the very edge of the porch. "Now, ask me who she is."

His demand was met with silence from Wolf and Neptune, and Blade allowed it for a moment before roaring down at the two men on their knees, making it clear who he was addressing. "Ask me. Ask me who she is."

Neptune's captive opened his mouth, silently gawping like a fish on a hook. Wolf's man glared up at him, his face a wash of crimson.

Blade rocked back on his heels, then forwards, letting gravity take hold, running down the steps in a rush, skidding to a stop in front of the men. They both flinched back as he reached for their throats, fingers of each hand finding the desired mark, his thumbs digging in deep and cutting off all air. They struggled, but with Wolf and

Neptune standing on the ropes anchoring their legs together, they never had a chance of escaping. Not really.

"*Ask. Me.*" He bent at the waist, shoving his face close to theirs as he relaxed his grip slightly, granting them the ability to pull in a shallow breath. "Fuckin' *ask* me."

"Who is she?" Neptune's man finally found his voice, and Blade focused his attention on him.

"She's mine." He clamped back down, watching as the men's faces turned red, then purple, eyes bulging in their sockets as they struggled for air. For life.

In the end, it was Jenn who saved them, even if they'd never know. Her face, as he'd seen her only hours ago, flashed through his thoughts. Soft, sweet, staring up at him from the pillow with that just-kissed haze she wore so well. So beautiful, and all his. The idea that he'd be touching her tonight with these same hands made him pull back. With clenched fists on his hips, he watched the two men heave and retch, writhing on the ground in front of him.

"Prez." This was off-script, and he didn't know if Gibby would give him this or not. After all was said and done, the Borderline Freaks MC weren't an outlaw crew, not really. They didn't fly the diamond and didn't refer to themselves as one-percenters. But to protect the club, to protect the life, he thought he could talk Gibby into the idea.

"Yeah, brother?" Blade turned to see Gibby'd taken a seat on the top step and was meticulously cleaning under his nails with the tip of a blade. He'd paused and looked up, his shaggy salt-and-pepper hair hanging low over one eye. "Whatcha need, man?"

"We cut 'em." Gibby nodded. "We called around." Another nod, slower as Gibby tried to follow Blade's logic. "Made a statement." No response this time, no reaction. "A short-term statement. I think we need something that'll last a fuck of a lot longer."

Gibby lifted his chin as he folded the naked blade back into the handle and shoved it into his pocket. "Whatcha thinkin', brother?"

"Give 'em a long-lasting anti-patch." He flicked a finger at a leather rectangle sewn to his vest. Positioned over his heart, it featured the initials that made up the club's name. BFMC. "Pair this with an interdictory circle. Makes a statement of not just no, but fuck no." These coveted patches were made in batches here at the clubhouse, using blank leather and a branding iron, and were only given to a member when they'd reached their second year with the club. He noted the instant when Gibby put it all together, and instead of the flinch he expected, he saw a steely resolve instead.

"Vote." Without another word, Gibby stood and lifted a hand, fist in the air. "All who want to brand these motherfuckers with a BFMC fuck no, so indicate."

Blade turned and looked around the group of men, inner circle and longtime members all. Along with his, every fist was raised.

"Mister Secretary, do you note the vote?" That was Neptune calling out as his role demanded.

Wolf answered quickly. "So noted, all ayes. Motion passes, and these motherfuckers are about to enter the entirety of the world of hurt."

Things happened quickly after that—the tiny charcoal stove brought out along with the long-handled brand. Blade watched as Monk and another member improvised a circle with a line across it, the internationally recognized symbol for no.

The men—Blade realized he'd stopped referring to them by name, even in his head—pleaded and screamed, and Wolf's man passed out when the red-hot iron touched the inside of his bicep, but in the end, it was done in two passes. First for the indelible mark of the club, and secondly the overlay of what they'd all started calling the Fuck No.

Blade watched as Gibby got in the men's faces, and whatever his whispered threats were, they were dire enough to make both men pale even further. Gibby then assigned two members to take the men back to their homes. They stood as a group, as a club, and watched the van drive away, carrying a cargo of rejects. Only when it was gone from sight did Gibby turn to Blade with his hand out. Blade offered his hand and quickly found himself pulled into a tight clinch, Gibby's mouth near his ear as he gave Blade the best advice he'd ever received.

"Just like with any tough mission, you had an objective. You reached that objective tonight, brother. Find and neutralize the threat to your woman's happiness. Mission fuckin' accomplished, man. Now, you're gonna think about those two asswipes, and you're gonna see them because it's not a large town, and when that happens, all you're gonna remember is two things. You ready? Wanna know what they are?" Gibby pulled back, studying him until Blade nodded and Gibby made a pleased sound. "First is you protected the club. With fire in your eyes, you fuckin' protected the goddamned club and I'm proud to call you mine. Fuckin' proud, brother. Second is you protected your woman. Not from the asswipes, but from you. You went to battle with yourself tonight, and you fuckin' won. Others will see her as your weakness, but you and I know different, don't we? She's not a weakness at all, not your soft belly spot, oh no. She's your strength, because you'll twist yourself into a fuckin' knot to be what she needs you to be. Well done, my brother. *Never forget what you did tonight.* Mission accomplished."

Blade held on for a moment more, eyes clenched tight against the flood of hot tears that threatened. When he had himself under lock and key, had his shit right and tight, he cleared his throat and gave Gibby the one word that meant the world. "Brother."

Fifteen

Jenn

The warm, familiar body slipping into bed woke Jenn. She rolled towards Blade and snuggled into his side as he wrapped an arm around her. Nose pressed to his ribs, she drew in a lungful of her flowery shower gel. Laughing softly, she touched his skin with her lips.

"What's so funny?" He didn't sound tired. There was a hard tone in his voice, an edge she hadn't heard before.

She blinked, the dim light in the room putting the time at long before her alarm would sound. "You showered." Nose brushing along his ribs, she smiled. "And now you smell like lilies." Another soft kiss to his skin. "Like me."

"Didn't take the time to unpack. My shit for the bathroom yet."

A shiver traveled through her at the brittle-sounding words. She lifted her head to look at him. Eyes open, he was staring at the ceiling, not even glancing at her as she moved. The expression he wore was fierce, and it looked as if he were raging internally.

"Blade?" She crowded closer and rested her palm on his chest. "What's goin' on?"

"Nate." At her question, he dipped his chin to his neck, staring at her. "Call me Nate when we're here, please."

"Okay." The idea he needed to create a separation between his club persona and the man she slept with actually sounded like a good idea, and she'd already started that with her insistence on using his name when they made love. "I can do that."

"Thanks, honey." His chin lifted, and he stared at the ceiling again.

"Nate." She smiled when he angled his head to look at her and repeated her question. "What's goin' on?"

"Jesus." He didn't sound aggrieved, just amused, and she let her grin grow broader. "Persistent little thing, aren't you?" He shifted around and up onto a hip, curving himself around her as he pulled her down against his chest. "There are going to be times when all I can tell you is that whatever's bothering me is club business. When that happens, you gotta let it lay. Club business is the equivalent of a nondisclosure. Confidential information I'm not at liberty to share. I'm bothered tonight and you caught wind of that, but that's all I can give you."

"You bothered is me bothered." Brows drawn together, she stared up at him. "I don't care about the club. I care about you."

"Honey, I am the club." She shook her head involuntarily at his words, not understanding. "It took me nearly two years total to earn my patch, because I took my time. I was unwilling to jump into something without a complete understanding. Two years where nearly everything I did was for the club, wedging my way into the corners of business and learning the men." He took a deep breath. "When I got out of the Marines, I was lost. Gibby and the brothers brought me a thing, a structure and brotherhood I needed. I'd have become a statistic, otherwise. I know it. Those were dark days. BFMC is a lot like the corps to me. Once a Marine, always a Marine, and likewise with the Borderline Freaks. So you sayin' you don't care about the club, that'll have to be something you come to terms with, because I am the club."

She studied his face, seeing nothing except a patient willingness to explain until she understood. If the club was that tied up in his personality, he was right, she had to care. Even if that meant abiding by some archaic gag order when it came to whatever had him troubled tonight. This felt like a watershed moment, where if she chose wrongly everything would come tumbling down around them. *I choose him*. And if that equated to the club, she'd find a way to be okay with that.

"Okay, Nate." Jenn dropped her head to rest on the pillow of his arm, pressing a kiss against it before looking up at him. "As long as you promise to tell me what I *can* do, then I'll do my best to not trespass where you don't want."

"It's not trespassing to ask what's wrong." He moved closer, lips hovering over hers. "That's you givin' a shit about me."

"I do give a shit." She angled her chin and brushed a soft kiss across his mouth.

"You wanna know what you can do?"

She nodded and smiled, already anticipating the answer. His arms tightened around her, and they rolled, him on top as he kissed her deep and slow, his tongue gliding along her lips before spearing into her mouth.

"Love me."

She kissed him back, hands slipping up along his sides until she clutched at his shoulders, pulling him down. His growing erection pressed against her hip, hot and hard. In a synchronized movement, he shifted on top of her as her legs spread, and Nate slotted between her thighs, pressing tight.

"I already do."

Sixteen

Blade

"Lucked out, brother." Blade smiled at Monk's words, eyes fixed across the yard filled with people and on his woman. Jenn sat at a picnic table with another member's daughter, their heads thrown back with laughter.

"I know it. Don't I just know it."

He couldn't tear his gaze from her. She'd slotted him into her life so easily, effortlessly. Already knew a bunch of his brothers from the diner, so hadn't exhibited any nervousness about coming to the pig roast today. She'd cooked yesterday, making a homemade potato salad he could attest was delicious, and hadn't hesitated loading the food into the car a prospect drove this morning, her house—*their* house—one of many on the man's route.

That tug he'd felt the first time he'd seen her had only grown, pulling him in until she was his world and he circled her, making sure she was safe and happy. The incident with the ex-prospects was weeks in the past, and he'd had dozens of nights sleeping by her side and waking up with her. She didn't grouse about the club, didn't begrudge him time to spend with his brothers, but also didn't hesitate to give him shit about other things, so he knew she wasn't just holding back.

Perfect.

"How's Amanda?"

He didn't miss the tiny smile Monk ducked his head to hide. After the last anniversary of Amanda's husband's death, apparently she and Monk had become friends on social media and were now constantly chatting. After a couple of years of seeing her from a distance, Monk was finally getting a chance to view things close-up, and he didn't seem to be put off by what she was showing him.

"She's good. I'm leavin' a little early today. She wants to go for a ride after she gets off work." Blade studied his friend, seeing only positive differences in him. Shoulders back, Monk seemed to stand taller, head held higher, and Blade liked seeing it.

"I approve, you know. Just in case you were wondering." He sensed Monk moving but didn't glance at him, fixing his attention back on Jenn.

"Wasn't asking your approval." Blade didn't respond, waiting, and Monk eventually gave it. "But I appreciate the gesture, brother."

"Anytime."

Jenn reached up and flipped the tail of her long, dark braid over her shoulder, worked her fingers through the tangled end as she listened to the chatter of a growing gaggle of women. Her friend Rose had arrived not long ago and was seated next to Jenn, but that woman's attention wasn't on the women around her. Blade followed her gaze and saw Wolf off to the side, talking to his ex-wife. They were standing close, and Wolf laughed and wrapped his arms around her, pulling her to his chest. Blade glanced back at Rose in time to see her face grow pale. She stood, said something to Jenn, who frowned in response but nodded, and walked around the far end of the clubhouse. A moment later he heard an engine start; then the sound dwindled to nothing. She'd left.

He looked back to Jenn to see her still frowning, her attention now on Wolf. His ex was walking away with a wave, but Wolf was already turned away, scanning the crowd of women.

"Monk, hey Monk." Instead of wincing as he would have at the need in his voice a year ago, he held his peace until

Monk responded with a grunt he took as a request to continue. "Life is fuckin' good, you know?"

"Yeah, brother. It really is."

"Gonna go see if my old lady's hungry yet." He angled his head and winked at Monk, who laughed aloud.

"Brother, we just ate."

"Oh, my friend." He thumped Monk's shoulder with a closed fist. "Not that kind of hunger."

He was only halfway to Jenn when she looked up at him. A smile curled her lips, and she stood, speaking to the other woman without taking her gaze off Blade. When he stretched out his hand, she met it with hers and threaded their fingers together, palm-to-palm. With catcalls and grins, his brothers waved them off.

On the bike, he paused and leaned back, pressing close for a moment just to feel the heat of her body against him. "Hey, Jenn?"

Chin propped on his shoulder, she asked, "What?"

"We get home, you're gettin' lucky." Their helmets clacked together as he turned his head. As expected, she had a wide grin on her face.

"Oh, I am? Am I?" She scooted a little closer, arms around his waist. "Lucky, huh?"

"Oh, yeah." He covered her hand with his, giving her fingers a squeeze. "So lucky."

"Means you're gettin' lucky too, you horn dog."

He toed the shifter down and into gear, nodding as he rolled them through the lot and onto the road, the bike's headlight illuminating the white line dashed into the distance.

Oh, yeah, he thought. *I'm so fuckin' lucky.*

~~~
~~~

THANK YOU SO MUCH FOR READING
More Than Enough!

This story is book #2 in the Borderline Freaks MC series, and is best enjoyed as a prelude to book #3, *Lack of In-between*. Featuring Wolf and Rose, that story is a testimony to the strength these characters showed me.

ABOUT THE AUTHOR

Raised in the south, *Wall Street Journal* & *USA TODAY* bestselling author MariaLisa learned about the magic of books at an early age. Every summer, she would spend hours in the local library, devouring books of every genre. Self-described as a book-a-holic, she says "I've always loved to read, but then I discovered writing, and found I adored that, too. For reading...if nothing else is available, I've been known to read the back of the cereal box."

Want sneak peeks into what she's working on, or to chat with other readers about her books? Join the Facebook group! **bit.ly/deMora-FB-group**

deMora's got a spam-free newsletter list she'd love to have you join, too: **bit.ly/mldemora-newsletter**

~~~~~
~~~~~

Borderline Freaks MC series

This series is comprised of four stories, and are best read in order to avoid spoilery situations.

Service and Sacrifice

"Thank you for your service" is what we're taught to say to military men and women in gratitude for our freedoms won at their expense. Less often do we thank their families, those left behind to hold down the fort, to manage the day-to-day struggle of keeping everything up in the air until their loved one returns.

When you can't count on anyone else to save you, there's only one real choice.

Amanda lost her husband to war. Alex lost part of himself. Through a series of glancing encounters, Amanda and Alex find reasons to continue on. And together, they'll discover hope and peace can be found in the most unexpected of places.

books2read.com/serviceandsacrifice

~~~

More Than Enough

When a man sees himself as damaged, imperfect, and flawed, it's hard to believe there could be love in his future. After a near-fatal accident stripped Blade of his confidence, he didn't hold out much hope … for anything.
~~~

Until Jenn—gorgeous, sweet, and kind—dropped into his life.

Where he sees destruction, she sees perfection.

Where he sees helplessness, she sees courage.

Where he sees ruin, she sees strength.

Can he ever believe he's more than enough?

books2read.com/morethanenough

~~~

Lack of In-between

Wolf finds Rose harbors more secrets than he expected, and the deeper he pulls her into his life, the more he likes it.

Once a man's been embedded in the bloody aftermath of battle after battle, with no relief in sight, he's forever changed.

Wolf came home from overseas to find his world askew. He was no longer a husband, since he and his ex agreed they were better friends than partners. But he still held the coveted position of father, an experience so confusing and rewarding it sometimes left him breathless.
~~~

He's got a lot on his plate personally, and even more with the Borderline Freaks and the challenges he and his club brothers have hit lately.

He just doesn't have time to make room for a relationship.

Right?

books2read.com/lackofinbetween

~~~

See You in Valhalla

This is Angelo Dobbs' worst nightmare. A good man lies dead, and with their president and founding member gone, the leadership position within the Borderline Freaks MC falls to him.

It's not that he can't manage the easy task of leading a group of good men; he would just have preferred to stay a little farther out of the spotlight. But, when his brothers issue the call, he answers.

Carly Gibson, daughter of his dead friend, is an unexpected—but not unwelcome—complication for his new role. She's the most intriguing woman he's ever met, capable and filled with a strength of character. He finds himself instinctively drawn to her. Could he have found the woman meant to complete him, finally?
~~~

Over the past couple of years, Dobbs, Neptune to the men of the BFMC, has watched as his closest friends found their soulmates. Now, their women are an integral part of the club, and when they and Carly are threatened, Neptune will do anything to ensure their safety—and just maybe, his future.

books2read.com/seeyouinvalhalla

Other Motorcycle Club Romance Series

My Rebel Wayfarers MC and the Neither This Nor That MC series do cross over, along with the Occupy Yourself band books, so readers have a couple of choices. The series can be read independently beginning with RWMC, OYBS, and then NTNT without too many spoilers. There's also a crossover between my RWMC world and Lila Rose's Hawks MC world. Or they can be read intertwined—in chronological order.

Here's the recommended reading order if you want to follow according to timing:

Mica, RWMC #1

A Sweet & Merry Christmas, RWMC #1.5

Slate, RWMC #2

Bear, RWMC #3

Born Into Trouble, OYBS #1

Jase, RWMC #4

Gunny, RWMC #5

Mason, RWMC #6

Hoss, RWMC #7

This Is the Route of Twisted Pain, NTNT #1

Harddrive Holidays, RWMC #7.5

Duck, RWMC #8

Biker Chick Campout, RWMC #8.5

Watcher, RWMC #9

Treading the Traitor's Path: Out Bad, NTNT #2

Living Without, Lila Rose's Hawks MC: Caroline Springs #4

Shelter My Heart, NTNT #3

A Kiss to Keep You, RWMC #9.25

Gun Totin' Annie, RWMC #9.5

Secret Santa, RWMC #9.75

Trapped by Fate on Reckless Roads, NTNT #4

Bones, RWMC #10

Gunny's Pups, RWMC #10.25

Not Even A Mouse, RWMC #10.75

Road Runner's Ride, RWMC #12.5

Never Settle, RWMC #10.5

Fury, RWMC #11

Christmas Doings, RWMC #11.25

Gypsy's Lady, RWMC #11.5

Thunderstruck, NTNT #5

Going Down Easy

No Man's Land

Cassie, RWMC #12

<div align="center">~~~~~</div>

Also by MariaLisa deMora

Neither This Nor That MC romance series

Legends are born from moments like these. Folktales spun around a single point in time so perfect, you can almost hear the click resonating through the universe as things align. Meet Twisted, Po'Boy, Retro, and Ragman, good old boys from southern states who have many things in common. First, is a bone-deep love of the biker lifestyle. Second, would be their love of the brotherhood, and knowing that you trust the man at your back. Finally, these men have the love of a good woman. None of these come without a price, and it is our pleasure to journey along with them as they discover the blessings that can be won, and lost along the way.

This is the Route of Twisted Pain
Treading the Traitor's Path: Out Bad
Shelter My Heart
Trapped by Fate on Reckless Roads
Thunderstruck

5-Star Reviews for the stories of the NTNT MC series

This is the Route of Twisted Pain

"This is the Route of Twisted Pain is an exhilarating, gripping romance novel contrived of incredible world building, complex yet relatable characters, and a unique, captivating plot.

Gifted storyteller MariaLisa deMora beautifully balances exciting suspense, fast action, intriguing secrets with delicious, blazing hot romance scenes.

Readers will be up all night with this riveting page-turner."

~ NY Literary Magazine

I am completely tickled in my fancy for TWISTED!

First off, let me state that there was one thing I didn't like about this book and that is the LAST PAGE! I hated for it to end. I dearly loved this book and its characters as well as their setting.

~Colleen M.

Gripping tale

Twisted and Penny fit together beautifully. The book covers so much more than just their love story. Great introduction to the Incoherent MC. The tale is gripping and gritty. The journey is full of twists and turns that keep you on the edge of your seat. I couldn't put it down. Cannot wait for the next one.

~Lillmil

Twisted is one of the most original and interesting characters I have read in a long time. Marialisa's character building is setting a high bar for her to follow, she will hopefully continue with Po'Boy's story. The Route of Twisted Pain was pure brilliance, and I highly recommend this read.
~Penny T.

This book obsessed me!
This may be the best book I read all year.
These people...they're not characters, they're real... have stuck in my head from the day I met them.
MariaLisa deMora can throw words down that'll Twist (hehe) your insides up till you can't breathe for waiting to hear what's next!
I'm working my way through her other 'families' and yup...she really is that good.
~DeLane

Treading the Traitor's Path: Out Bad

"Treading the Traitor's Path: Out Bad is a solidly engrossing, well-written novel by a talented author.
MariaLisa deMora delivers a thrilling ride filled with exciting suspense, deliciously explicit, vivid sex scenes, and gritty, fast-paced action. Her characters are smart, complex, and strong with sharp edges. The settings meticulously detailed.
Fans of Motorcycle Club romance stories will not want to miss this second installment in deMora's exciting series."
~ NY Literary Magazine

Book Hangover

What an amazing read! DeMora does not simply wrote a book, she pulls you into a different world. When you read her work, you are very much surrounded by the characters and setting. Prepare for a book hangover because once you finish the book, you will still be stuck with Po Boy.

~KW

More More More

THIS WAS AMAZING. Highly recommend for a good story line, interesting characters. I just wish there was more more more.

~Laura

Loved This Book!

What did I just read?! Is my kindle still working? I'm pretty sure it combusted into flames while reading this story. RED HOT READ for 2017. Not what I was expecting at all! I tend to stay away from ménage a trois, because for me it's hard to say there's any kind of conflict except for jealousy, and the ending kind of leaves things unresolved and unrealistic. NOT THIS BOOK! The best one out there guaranteed.

~Linda A

So Freaking Good

...seriously this series is just WTF so freaking good. Dark, Twisted, harsh, painful and raw. Po'Boy lives for his club, his brothers and his family, there is nothing he wouldn't do for them.

~Fay

The author delivers a 5-STAR READ
I live and breathe for books like this! Fabulously Naughty!...Wickedly Hot! This is my first book by MariaLisa deMora and it will not be my last. MariaLisa delivered a 5 STAR READ! The plot is filled with action, suspense, romance and tons of hot scenes.
~Jenny F
~~~~~
~~~~~

Alace Sweets, a dark romantic suspense standalone

A dark thriller, this book is not a light read. Filled with edge-of-your-seat suspense, this intense story commands the reader's attention as it drives towards the explosive ending. Alace Sweets is a vigilante serial killer, with everything that implies and is sure to trip all your triggers. Be ready.

At seventeen, Alace Sweets turned a corner in her life, taking the wrong shortcut home from school.

Resisting the harsh knowledge her attackers will never be made to pay for their actions, Alace takes a stand. Justice must be served, and if fate's scales are out of balance, she's determined to set things right as best she can.

When the laws of men fail, the rules of Alace prevail.

5-Star Reviews for Alace Sweets

"Whatever deep dark trench [deMora] pulled a character like Alace from should be revisited again and often."
~Confessions of a Serial Reader

"Thrilling...chilling...full of suspense, nail biting edge of your seat excitement."
~Tracey H

"Every time MariaLisa deMora picks up her pen (or opens her computer), she creates characters you want to believe in."
~Gail S

"Intriguing dark storyline, beautiful love story and nail-biting conclusion, what more could a reader ask for?"
~Manda M

"This book takes you a dark and twisted ride that is gripping..."
~Renee Entress' Blog

"This book is dark and gritty and I literally had to take a day off from reading it because it's that intense."
~My Girlfriend's Couch

"This is my favourite book so far from this author ... I recommend this book if you enjoy dark romantic thrillers."
~Cheekypee Reads and Reviews

"There's not enough stars to give this book and 5 just doesn't really do it justice!"
~DeLane C

"I couldn't put this book down from page one! Tried to stop & go to bed but couldn't sleep thinking about Alace and got up & finished the book."
~Debbie M

"MariaLisa DeMora, wordsmith that she is, made this a story of the enlightenment of a woman and finding love in a life where she has had none."
~Kat W

~~~~~
~~~~~

Hard Focus, a criminal thriller standalone

This is an intense page-turner, a gut-punch twist-filled story about a woman who has confidence in herself, believes she's a good judge of character, and has filled her life with people she can trust. She's right, but she's also very, very wrong. Readers will have a time of it trying to decide who to watch closest.

Where do you place your trust when your own instincts betray you?

Connie Rowe is a receptionist at a respected legal firm. She's a little bit sassy, a lotta bit happy, has good friends, and is adored by her neighbors.

Life is good.

She's got a boyfriend she enjoys spending time with. He can be a little intense, but he's got a lot going on in his own life, sorting out his young daughter and nightmare of an ex.

Life is grand.

"Trust your gut." That's what Connie's police officer father told her often, training his daughter to believe in herself through the years.

But … what happens when you can't? When your intuition lies?

What happens when things come into Hard Focus?

5-Star Reviews for Hard Focus

"Hard Focus is one very well-written tale. 5 stars is not enough for me."
~Tabitha

"What a powerful story. [deMora] kept me invested from the first word to the last."
~Jesse R

"[deMora] has a certain magical touch to writing her characters, that they become either your nemesis, your best friend, or your love interest. That is certainly portrayed in this spin around. Loved it, loved it, loved it."
~Sandy K

"I strongly recommend this book for both entertainment and to broaden your knowledge of certain laws that must be revisited."
~Words Turn Me On

"An intense page turner. Once you start, you can't put the book down."
~Tracey H

"A beautifully written, powerful read that I can't rate highly enough. This story will stay with me always."
~Gayle

"This book had twists I didn't see coming. Loved it!"
~Lori R

"Wow! I am in awe of deMora's skill in crafting this story."
~Kat W

"I keep sayin that there just aren't enough stars to give to some of Marialisa deMora's books...this one is no different!"
~DeLane

"Where do I start with this one...I read this in 3 1/2 hours uninterrupted, I absolutely could NOT put it down. Very deep, keeps you guessing, what's gonna happen next, kind of book. I love how strong her characters are, especially the females!"
~Wendy I

"Sometimes I feel like MariaLisa deMora is the one I should be watching out for. I started reading her books because I'm addicted to MC Romance, but then she decides to change things up and I just follow her wherever she leads me like a Pied Piper. I never know what to expect, and sometimes I'm afraid to find out, but it's always an adventure."
~Rosa for iScream Books Blog

"A plot full of twists and turns, a story that's not quite what it seems, strong characterization, jaw dropping revelations... what more do you need from a book?"
~Manda M

"This book kept me turning the pages wondering what was going to happen. I am usually pretty good at guessing twists but not with this book. She totally surprised me and brought me out of my funk. 5 stars."
~Glenna M

"What an amazing story! Filled with a smidge of suspense, a dash of action and a heap of realism of our country's laws and how their vague application to victims can adversely affect its citizens and the people in their lives."
~Naughty Mom Story Time

ADDITIONAL SERIES AND BOOKS

Please note that books in a series frequently feature characters from additional books within that series. If series books are read out of order, readers will twig to spoilers for the other books, so going back to read the skipped titles won't have the same angsty reveals.

Rebel Wayfarers MC series:

Mica, #1
A Sweet & Merry Christmas, #1.5
Slate, #2
Bear, #3
Jase, #4
Gunny, #5
Mason, #6
Hoss, #7
Harddrive Holidays, #7.5
Duck, #8
Biker Chick Campout, #8.5
Watcher, #9
A Kiss to Keep You, #9.25
Gun Totin' Annie, #9.5
Secret Santa, #9.75
Bones, #10
Gunny's Pups, #10.25
Never Settle, #10.5
Not Even A Mouse, #10.75
Fury, #11
Christmas Doings, #11.25
Gypsy's Lady, #11.5
Cassie, #12
Road Runner's Ride, #12.5

Occupy Yourself band series:

Born Into Trouble, #1
Grace In Motion, #2 (TBD)
What They Say, #3 (TBD)

Neither This, Nor That MC series:

This Is the Route Of Twisted Pain, #1
Treading the Traitor's Path: Out Bad, #2
Shelter My Heart, #3
Trapped by Fate on Reckless Roads, #4
Thunderstruck, #5

**Rebel Wayfarers & Incoherent MC
(NTNT) crossover stories:**

Going Down Easy
No Man's Land

Mayhan Bucklers MC series:

Most Rikki-Tik, #1
Mad Minute, #2
Pucker Factor, #3
Boocoo Dinky Dau, #4 (TBD)

Borderline Freaks MC series:

Service and Sacrifice, #1
More Than Enough, #2
Lack of In-between, #3
See You in Valhalla, #4

If You Could Change One Thing:
Tangled Fates Stories

There Are Limits, #1
Rules Are Rules, #2
The Gray Zone, #3

Other Books:

With My Whole Heart
Bet On Us
Alace Sweets
Seeking Worthy Pursuits (TBD)
Hard Focus
Dirty Bitches MC: Season 3

More information available at **mldemora.com**.